Author portrait: Amy Arbus

Kate Jennings was raised near Griffith, New South
Wales. She now lives in New York City where she works
as a writer and editor. She has published a book of
poetry, *Come To Me My Melancholy Baby* (1975) and a
book of essays, *Save Me, Joe Louis* (1989). She also edited
Mother I'm Rooted, a landmark collection of poetry
by women.

OTHER BOOKS BY KATE JENNINGS

Come To Me My Melancholy Baby
Mother I'm Rooted (editor)
Save Me, Joe Louis

WOMEN FALLING DOWN IN THE STREET

STORIES

KATE JENNINGS

William Heinemann Australia

First published 1990 by
William Heinemann Australia
22 Salmon Street, Port Melbourne, Victoria 3207

Edited by Jamie Grant
Designed by Bob Cato
Typeset in 12/14 Garamond 3
by EMS (Evans Mason Services), Melbourne
Printed in Australia by Australian Print Group

National Library of Australia
  cataloguing-in-publication data:

Jennings, Kate, 1948-
  Women Falling Down In The Street.
  ISBN 0 85561 371 8.
  I. Title.
A823.3

The cover illustration is reproduced with the kind permission of the
artist, Oscar de Mejo, and Nahan Galleries.

For Bob Cato

ACKNOWLEDGEMENTS

'The Magazine for Pool Families' first appeared in *The Bulletin*,
'Yoo-Hoo' in *The Sydney Review*,
'Mapping Myself' in *Australia Short Stories No. 25*,
'Mistakes, Too Many To Mention', in *Island*,
'Samuel Beckett is Dead' in *Vogue*,
'Women Falling Down in the Street' in *GH*.
A shorter version of 'Breakfast in Fur'
appeared in the *Sydney Morning Herald*.

CONTENTS

BREAKFAST IN FUR

The first thing you notice about Oneida is her nose, knobbed at the bridge like the poet Anna Akhmatova's. After that, her clothes. I have only ever seen her in a loose, unevenly dyed black skirt, a pink 1950s cardigan with beading on the front, the kind currently back in vogue, and running shoes. This, I suspect, is her outfit for special occasions, which my meetings with her always are.

Oneida is an eccentric, the genuine item in that she says and does as she pleases and is indifferent to your opinion of her. Sometimes, from under her eccentricity, fear sticks out, like the shoes of a cartoon burglar protruding from behind a curtain. No doubt the fear comes from being sixty-three, alone, and poor. Fortunately Oneida isn't the sort to feel sorry for herself. At least she doesn't give that impression. Who knows? Maybe she is one of those who late at night dress up their regrets in grotesque costumes and set them to lumbering around the room on stilts.

Oneida is a photographer. She started out in New York at the end of the Second World War, showing her portfolio to the art directors of magazines at the time when Richard Avedon, Irving Penn, and Frank Scavullo were doing the same thing. Unlike them, Oneida has never had much success. This does not mean she lacks talent. On the contrary, she has the happy gift of bestowing on her subjects, even the shyest and dumbest of them, a curious cockeyed confidence, a certain sardonic knowingness, qualities Oneida happens to possess in abundance.

Talent she has but sell herself she can't. And Oneida knows it. In fact, she likes to tell stories about the artist Alice Neel, another of her acquaintances from those days immediately after the war. Alice Neel was a tireless self-promoter. Oneida, or so she says, made slides of Alice's paintings, and Alice carried them around in her handbag and would whip them out, along with a pocket viewer, for anyone who would stand still for a minute.

'The women's movement took up Alice Neel,' I once said to Oneida. 'Feminists love her lumpy-bodied women.'

'You mean Alice Neel took up the women's movement,' snorted Oneida, half in disgust and half in admiration.

Alice Neel came up again in the conversation we had the day we lunched in the members' dining room at the Museum of Modern Art. We sat at the back, up against Jasper Johns's map of the United States. Oneida was directly beneath the Florida panhandle and I was around about Louisiana. Oneida had wild mushrooms stuffed with Black Forest ham as an appetizer and duck salad with blueberry vinaigrette for her main course, followed by almond cake and cappuccino. Oneida cares as little for her figure as she does for clothes. I had a spinach omelette and decaffeinated coffee, no milk, no sugar, and spent the entire meal eyeing Oneida's sourdough roll, which for some reason she didn't eat. The museum's sourdough rolls are excellent.

I had heard a story the day before that I thought would appeal to Oneida, about Meret Oppenheim, the surrealist artist who did the famous fur-lined teacup on display on the second floor of the museum, the same floor we were dining on – in the room to the right as you come off the escalator, a work of art that gets your complete attention no matter how many times you have seen it because the idea is so simple and, well, surreal. Called 'Déjeuner en Fourrure' by Oppenheim, the fur-lined teacup is referred to in English variously as 'Breakfast in Fur', 'Luncheon in Fur', and 'Dinner in Fur'. Apparently it brings to mind another meal altogether for lesbians, who view it as a sexual symbol. I have noticed the museum go out of their way to avoid references to meals of any sort by labelling it 'Object'.

Oppenheim was twenty-three when she created her 'Déjeuner en Fourrure', much younger than any of the male surrealists. Alas, for the next eighteen years she destroyed or left unfinished everything she did, and came to speak eloquently, as might be expected, on the problems confronting women artists.

My flippant comment about Alice Neel and the women's movement might have caused you to think I am unsympathetic to feminist issues. Untrue. After all, I am forty years old, and women who reach that age and are still suspicious of feminism have to be wearing blinkers meant for a cart horse. By the time a woman gets to Oneida's age, any residual illusions about who is running the show and the interests they have at heart will have been stripped clean away.

'The men. Have you been watching them on television?' I had asked Oneida at the beginning of our lunch, referring to the Iran-Contra hearings. Day after day a parade of Democrats, Republicans, lawyers, and subpoenaed witness, all men with the notable exception of Fawn Hall, had been strutting their stuff, less interested in justice than with impressing their peers. Almost blowing kisses at each other.

'Which men?' countered Oneida, and then, quick as a flash, 'Oh, *those* men.' Enough said. Subject closed.

Meret Oppenheim looked a little like Picasso, only taller because she had a neck. She also had class. One day in a café on the Left Bank, a businessman, a typical bourgeois, waistcoat stretched across fat stomach, cigar clamped in mouth, black homburg on his head, was railing loudly against artists and their slovenly, freeloading ways. Oppenheim went up to him, took off his hat, and placed it on the floor. Then, cool as you please, she squatted down and peed in it. This was the story I told Oneida, feeling rather pleased with myself as I did so.

Oneida gave a cackle, but a half-hearted one, because she wanted to tell a story of her own, an Alice Neel story. In her old age, Alice, feted and acclaimed at last, was invited to a college to give a talk. At the reception party in the dean's office, with everybody standing around exchanging politenesses, Alice asked the whereabouts of the toilet. Down the hall and to the right, replied the dean. That's too far, said Alice, and spread her legs and urinated on the carpet.

Although I was peeved Oneida had one-upped me, I marvelled at Alice Neel's audacity, if that is the word for it. We should collaborate on a book about outrageous women, I proposed to Oneida, but again she was not really listening. She had another story to tell, completely unrelated and one which she obviously intended to be the centrepiece of the lunch. I settled back to listen.

'Judith from the temp agency phoned me a few weeks back. Nice gal. Wanted to know if I was interested in a couple of days work with the Mitsubishi Bank,' Oneida began.

'What could you do for them? Publicity photos?'

'No. Typing.'

'Typing? You type? In an office?' I was so surprised I forgot my manners. I could sooner imagine Arnold Schwarzenegger in a typing pool than Oneida. It seems, though, she fairly jumped at the temp agency's offer. A chance to observe some Japanese close up, she explained. Everything about them fascinated her. Not the same as going to Japan, of course, but it would suffice.

At the Mitsubishi Bank, Oneida was shown to her desk in the typing pool, a football field of grey carpet lit by merciless fluorescence. To her disappointment, the other desks were filled with Americans. 'Gum-chewing girls from Brooklyn,' she sniffed. 'Low-necked blouses. And ankle bracelets under their stockings. You know. Stuffed toys and pictures of their boyfriends in plastic heart-shaped frames all over the place.' Only the supervisor was Japanese, a timid woman not worthy of study in Oneida's opinion.

Later, sent on an errand by the supervisor, Oneida set off down a corridor – more grey carpet and fluorescent glare – and was soon lost. Unable to find anyone to ask the way, she opened a door experimentally. Lo and behold, there they were. Japanese, lots of them, neat as pins and industrious as could be.

'Different air to breathe,' said Oneida.

As Oneida was leaving for the day, the supervisor took her aside. Apparently she was impressed by Oneida's work. Would she consider a regular job with the bank?

Oneida drew herself up. 'I would not,' she replied. 'I am an *irregular* person.'

Arriving with time to spare the next morning, Oneida decided to explore. This time she got well and truly lost. She bounced along empty corridors for at least ten minutes before finally opening another door. And found herself in a boardroom. First she inspected the furniture – 'The Japanese do wonderful things with wood.' – and was getting around to the paintings – 'Abstract Expressionists. A lot of Clyfford Still. Very showy.' – when a Japanese materialized at her side.

'Oh, he was beautiful,' said Oneida, shaking her head at the memory. 'He was…' she struggled to find the right word, '…a *princeling*! Everything perfect. His haircut. His tie. Snowy shirt. His shoes. All perfect.' Oneida was entranced.

The 'princeling' stared at Oneida, and she stared right back. It was becoming obvious he was angry. In fact, his face was turning crimson with rage. When the Japanese stop being excruciatingly polite and show their displeasure, they can really lose their lolly.

'What are you doing here!?' The whole sentence

was a yelp. 'This is *management*.' Oneida started to try to placate him but thought better of it. Slowly he raised an outstretched arm to shoulder height, index finger pointing to the door. Oneida admired his impeccably manicured nails. 'Exit!'

Oneida exited. Back at the typing pool, she found the supervisor waiting for her. The supervisor was crying silently, tears slipping down her face.

'You have to leave,' she said to Oneida.

'Now? This very minute?'

'Yes.' The supervisor looked about ready to expire from shame. The phone rang. 'I can't talk,' she said in a pained whisper to the person on the other end. 'She's still here.' And started to cry again.

After the supervisor had put the phone down, Oneida asked, 'Will you pay me for today?'

'Yes. And tomorrow. And the day after.'

'Marvellous,' said Oneida.

Going down the escalator after lunch, Oneida told me she had taken the job with the bank so she could pay for a consultation with a psychiatrist.

'I've been a bit depressed lately,' she confided. After listening to Oneida for a session, the pyschiatrist had said to her, 'You know, Oneida, you've lived your life by fluke.'

The word 'fluke' must have caught Oneida's fancy because right there on the escalator she let loose a high-pitched giggle and shouted 'Fluke!' as if it were a battle cry. Everyone turned and stared.

Subdued, she added, 'But I knew that already.'

Hugs and kisses outside the museum, and Oneida headed in the direction of Sixth Avenue, and I of Fifth.

· · ·

Oneida was waiting for me on the corner of Madison
and Seventy-second. It was four months since we had
seen each other. Padded out by winter clothes, Oneida
looked rounder than I remembered. Her hair had been
cropped to stubble. And with those sly eyes, right
away I thought: Gertrude Stein.

'I've been in the hospital!' Oneida shouted as soon
as she spotted me.

'Oh no! What was wrong?' I shouted back.

'Nothing! I was in the hospital because I'm
healthy.' As we walked up Madison, she explained
how she had been in the hospital for two weeks as part
of a study to do with Alzheimer's disease. Doctors had
wanted to compare someone with the disease against a
control, someone who was normal.

'You normal!' I kidded her. We reached Sant
Ambroeus, the café where we were to have afternoon
tea. My treat. The ceilings and walls of Sant Ambroeus
are swagged with silk cloth, but instead of feeling
lapped by luxury, the effect the decor is supposed to
induce, we were both immediately overcome by claus-
trophobia. Because of this, I asked if we could be
seated out in the middle of the room. The tables there
are about three inches apart. I hoped Oneida would
keep her voice down.

Our waiter had ginger hair and pink cheeks and
wore his homosexuality as if it were braiding on an
officer's uniform. Oneida gave him a huge smile. Sant
Ambroeus is not the kind of café where patrons smile
at the waiters. He responded in kind.

'I'm in love,' said Oneida, indicating the depart-
ing waiter. 'Not like I love Regis. Regis I love forever.
But for the moment.' Regis is my boyfriend.

Oneida ordered coffee-flavoured gelato and an

espresso, and I Darjeeling tea and a slice of fruit tart. Oneida's order came almost immediately, but was not served as expected. The gelato was in a brandy balloon, the espresso in a small jug, and the waiter, hamming it up for Oneida, poured the espresso over the gelato with an exaggerated flourish. It steamed.

Between mouthfuls, she waved her hand at me. 'D'you like it?' She was wearing an inexpensive digital watch with a bright red band. Oneida was as pleased as punch with this watch. She had just come from Bloomingdale's, where she was given it as a re-placement for a faulty watch she had bought there the day before. The second watch retailed for more than the first, so that was why she was pleased.

'Tell me about the hospital, Oneida.'

'It was paradise. I had my own room. The nurses brought me meals on a tray. And I was paid seventy dollars a day. But some of the procedures they did on me weren't easy. They would put IV needles in both arms and leave them there for eight hours. One procedure they took blood every five minutes.' While she talked, she admired her new watch, angling it this way and that.

'They made you work for your seventy dollars,' I said, upset that Oneida was reduced to doing things like this to support herself.

'It wasn't as bad as at Columbia Presbyterian. They were conducting an experiment on schizophrenia and wanted normal people for that too. The subjects had to have their heads shaved and then they were put in a machine and X-rayed.'

I took in Oneida's cropped hair again, this time with alarm. 'You did that?'

Oneida laughed. 'No. I decided against it. This is

just the way I had my hair cut.' She ran her hand over what was left of her hair, feeling its texture. 'One of the procedures in the Alzheimer's study was a spinal tap. The doctor who took me through the whole protocol said the spinal tap was optional but to remember I'd be doing it for humanity. No way, I told him, not even for humanity.' Oneida was enjoying bandying around words like 'protocol' and 'procedure'.

'I should hope you didn't,' I said.

'I brought you something. A compote. Let me give it to you before I forget.' Oneida produced a crumpled paper bag and handed it to me. 'I made it myself. You know what I put in it? I went to Zabar's and bought dried cherries.'

I peered into the bag. It contained a jar of stewed fruit. I thanked Oneida and put it on the table.

Oneida snuck another look at her watch. She did a double-take. 'Oh no!' She took the watch off, put it to her ear, shook it. 'This watch is no good either. It still says four o'clock.' She handed it across to me. I held it to my ear. No ticking. Then I remembered it was a quartz watch and wouldn't tick even when it was working.

Oneida leaned across to the couple at the next table and asked them if they knew anything about watches. The couple, who were both wearing Cartier tank watches, shifted in their seats away from Oneida. They politely told her they didn't. She told them the story of the watch, how it was a replacement for one she had bought the day before. 'D'you think there is something wrong with me?' she asked them.

'You'll have to take it back to Bloomingdale's,' I said.

Oneida became distraught. 'I hate going to

Bloomingdale's. It's like that Buñuel movie. The one where they can't leave the room.'

'*The Exterminating Angel.*' Oneida was trying to get me to go back to the store with her.

'Two watches in a row. What did I do to deserve this?'

I gave in. 'I'll come with you.'

She brightened. 'Will you, darling? That's lovely.'

The waiter had forgotten to bring my tea and fruit tart. I called him over. Oneida ordered some more coffee.

'He's cute, isn't he?' said Oneida. 'But the service would be better in one of those formica joints.' She took the linen napkin from off her lap and noisily blew her nose on it. This was done for the benefit of the people at the next table, who shifted in their seats again. Something was bothering Oneida; she was more manic than usual.

We sat in silence for a minute or two, Oneida giving the other customers the once-over. Then she said, 'I don't know anybody who is rich. Really rich, I mean. I do know someone who knows women who hang out with rich men. The bed business is supposed to be absolutely lousy.'

'Rich men are bad in bed?'

'Yeah. It's because their work is more exciting than sex. Ernest used to say that nothing can compare with having a power complex satisfied.'

'Who's Ernest?'

'My ex-husband.'

'You had a husband?'

'Only for a few years.'

'Tell me more. How did you meet him?'

'We met on the subway. He asked me some directions. It was during the war. The strangest people get together during war.' She hunched conspiratorially over the table. 'War is very sexy.'

'I've heard,' I said. 'What did Ernest do?'

'He was one of those brilliant people who don't want any responsibility, so he was always changing jobs. Last I heard of him he was working in a casino in Reno. I married him because I knew it wouldn't last. Up front there was an exit sign.' She interrupted herself. 'I just remembered. A couple of years ago I took some photographs of a woman married to a very rich man. He used to say, "Wear my fur coat tonight. And put my diamonds on I bought for you." That kind of thing. Her everything was his.'

I started to say something derogatory about kept women, but Oneida stopped me. 'Don't be so fast to criticize. Life is difficult. You pick your way to live it. Sometimes I say to myself, "Are you out of your mind? Are you totally crazy? Why did you not want to live on Park Avenue? Why didn't you marry a rich man?" But look at it this way. If I were married and living on Park Avenue, could I go live in the hospital for two weeks?' As far as I could tell Oneida wasn't joking.

Oneida abruptly changed gears. 'My sister died while I was in the hospital,' she blurted out.

'Oneida, I *am* sorry.' So that's what was wrong. Oneida had been close to her sister.

'It isn't like losing my parents. This is much harder. We grew up together.'

'A shared history.'

'You know what it feels like? An insult, a personal insult. But then I'm an egomaniac.'

This was bluster. I reached out and took Oneida's

hand and held it tight.

After she'd quietened, Oneida said, 'In the hospital, they were taking my blood pressure and pulse and temperature all the time. After my sister died, I asked the nurses if there was any change. But there wasn't.'

I looked around for the waiter. 'Oneida, can you see the waiter?'

'My redhead. Where is he? I think he went home.'

Eventually he reappeared. I signalled him to bring the bill. When it came, Oneida asked how much it was.

'Nineteen dollars,' I told her.

'I can't believe it,' she said. 'Next time I'm going to take you.'

While we were waiting for our coats, Oneida ran her eyes over the silk swagging. 'You know what this place reminds me of?' she said in a stage whisper. 'A coffin.'

It was already dark outside and had started to sleet. The road was made of black glass. We took a bus down to Bloomingdale's. The bus was crowded. Oneida and I were pushed up close together. Oneida smelled of wet wool.

The woman at the watch counter sent us to the repair department. All the watch needed was a new battery. We walked through the store to Third Avenue, where we boarded an uptown bus even more crowded than the one before. I clutched the compote in its paper bag to my chest, Oneida held onto my elbow. It was very hot in the bus. Our faces started to flush. Oneida, looking up at me, said, 'Don't you enjoy a bus ride?' And then, quite firmly, as if she were setting the record straight, 'I don't believe in generalities. I bet there are some tycoons who are good screws.'

THE MAGAZINE FOR
POOL FAMILIES

A Monday morning, grey in feel as Mondays in
Manhattan often are. The phone rings. Angel can't
place the woman on the other end. Then she remembers. A magazine editor, dreadfully stooped, the letter
S in a Victorian alphabet. They had worked together
years ago downtown. An incident from that time
comes immediately to mind. One evening, quite late,
thinking she was the last to leave the office, Angel had
switched off some hall lights. A terrible sound, more a
bellow than a scream, and the S-shaped editor came
rushing out of the gloom. 'The dark. I can't bear the
dark,' she said, her cheeks working. Now, on the
phone, the editor wants to know if Angel would write
a piece for her on travelling alone. Angel says yes.

• • •

Angel phones her friend Vincenza. 'Any thoughts on

travelling alone?' she asks.

'I take a pillow from home with me,' says Vincenza.

'You carry a pillow? Isn't that, ah, cumbersome?'

'A small pillow. A baby one. I know someone who takes their own sheets with them.'

On a pad of yellow legal paper, Angel writes, 'Take own sheets.'

. . .

Angel has someone coming to dinner, a woman she met at a gallery opening. She had liked the way the woman talked, her careful sentences. Friendship is in the offing.

Angel opens the door. The woman is tiny. She has the bones of a bird. She is wearing jeans with high-heeled shoes, a sexy Chanel schoolgirl blouse, a cloth coat with a thick beaver collar. Angel realizes she has made a mistake.

Angel takes the coat, gets her guest a drink. They talk. Angel is doubly sure she has made a mistake. The woman's sentences are not so much careful as squeezed out.

For dinner, Angel serves a stew. She has rolled the cubes of meat in tomato paste and simmered them gently in a cup of dry red wine, along with onions, potatoes, carrots, a bay leaf, garlic, thyme. The woman breaks off a morsel of carrot with the edge of her fork, puts it in her mouth, sets down the fork, chews the carrot slowly, very slowly. She takes a sip of water, picks up the fork again, toys with some meat, doesn't actually eat any. She watches Angel's fork as it travels from the plate to Angel's mouth, laden with food.

Angel is sympathetic. She knows what it is like

to live on air and nothing else. She lived like that for years herself but woke up one day with an appetite and now she eats every last thing on her plate. Right now she wants to sop up the gravy with bread. She reaches for some bread, catches her guest watching her, thinks better of it.

The conversation lurches along. It dawns on Angel that the woman has no sense of humour. She approaches everything with the same undeviating seriousness, as if she were a soldier practising a bayonet charge.

The silences are becoming immense. Angel remembers her assignment from the morning.

'You travel a lot?'

'Yes,' says the woman.

'Alone?'

'Yes.'

'Do you do anything to make travelling alone easier?'

The woman looks puzzled. 'I don't find it difficult in the first place.'

She never calls to thank Angel for dinner.

. . .

On her way to the supermarket, Angel stops to post a letter at a mailbox on Lexington Avenue. She overhears a woman talking to her two dogs, silky-haired terriers with bright button eyes. She is asking them, 'What do *you* want to do today.'

At the supermarket check-out counter, Angel empties her basket. A packet of arrowroot biscuits. Six navel oranges. Strawberries. The woman in front of her, who is waiting for her change, lets out a squawk of indignation. She is pointing at a magazine in a display rack next to Angel. *Poolside*, it is called. *The magazine for pool families.* 'Do they think they are going to sell that here, in Manhattan? Who has a pool in Manhattan?' The woman collects her change and her bag of groceries and bangs out of the supermarket.

A block from the supermarket, a panhandler comes up to Angel, right up close until he is in her face. 'Hard time,' he says. 'Hard time.'

As she waits to cross the street, a man on the opposite pavement catches Angel's attention. He has a limp. One leg swings wide around in front of the other leg. A young woman comes down the street toward him. She has long blonde hair and is wearing a form-fitting black sweater and scarlet skirt. As she passes him, the man with a limp, the better to watch her, twists his torso, twists it until his head is almost facing backwards. His leg inscribes its arc.

· · ·

In a mood to count her blessings, Vincenza had told Angel, 'My life has been fortunate. Why, at one point I went through a stage of wanting good jewellery and I got it.' She laughed as she said this, mocking herself the way people who have a social conscience do when they admit to indulging themselves. Vincenza's husband had bought the jewellery for her. He likes to go to auctions at Christie's or Sotheby's, to see if he can pick up a bargain.

Vincenza is not so sanguine now. She and her husband have a house in the country on the Connecticut River. They worked hard to buy the land, build the house. The place means everything to them. Now the town council are claiming to be legally entitled to put in a road that will go smack through Vincenza's living room. At the end of the road, there will be a dock for speedboats, public toilets, a hotdog stand or two. They will probably have to sell Vincenza's jewellery to pay for a lawyer. Vincenza has taken to quoting Hobbes, saying life is nasty, brutish, and short.

Angel doesn't have any good jewellery, but she knows what Vincenza meant when she said she had gone through a stage of wanting some. While visiting Vincenza, she had come across a Christie's catalogue Vincenza's husband had left on the coffee table: *Item 308. Pair of diamond earrings. Each bezel-set with an old European-cut diamond atop a smaller European-cut diamond, mounted in white gold-topped yellow gold.* If I had those earrings, everything would be all right, she had said to herself. She didn't mean it, of course, not really.

Instead of working on her piece for the S-shaped editor, Angel goes to the Christie's auction. She signs up for a paddle, takes a seat. The auctioneer is up to item 196, stickpins in amusing shapes, a hare with a ruby eye, a camera with an emerald for a lens, a car with pearls for wheels and fenders of black onyx. Estimated to go for around $800, these trinkets are knocked down for $3,000.

'What can I tell you? They're going crazy. It's junk,' says the man behind her and leaves.

Eventually item 308 comes up. The auctioneer, a woman with prominent teeth and hooded eyes, opens the bidding at $900.

'Nine hundred and fifty. One thousand. One thousand one hundred. Two hundred. Three hundred. One thousand four hundred . . .' Angel feels like a runner who hasn't heard the starting gun. Before she even considers putting her paddle in the air, the auctioneer is saying, 'Any other interest at three thousand five hundred. Fair warning. Fair warning. All through at three thousand five hundred. In the middle of the room.'

Angel cranes to see the person in the middle of the room who bid for the earrings, but already everybody's attention is on the next item.

. . .

Angel goes to a party. A tall young man wearing a small straw hat on the back of his head introduces himself to her. He tells her he writes short stories and his hero is Raymond Carver. In fact, he has just come back from a trip to Carver Country.

'I met Tess Gallagher. She's very nice.' He says this shyly.

When she was twenty, Angel fell in love with a boy because he made a pilgrimage to e.e. cummings's grave. She likes that kind of gesture.

'Are you happy?' Angel asks him. She has had two glasses of wine and already is disposed to saying things she wouldn't ordinarily.

His big open face closes up. 'Yeah, I'm happy.' He pushes his hat even further back on his head. 'I know this is a corny question,' he continues, a little embarrassed by what he is about to say, 'but do you think it matters that I haven't had an unhappy life? A Carveresque life?'

'I don't think it matters,' says Angel. She has one more glass of wine and then goes home.

. . .

The next morning Angel begins her piece for the S-shaped editor. *These days everybody, not just the rugged*

*individualists among us, travels alone, off to the four corners
of the earth, briefcases in hand, backpacks slung in place,
trundling suitcases on little wheels...*

. . .

Angel lies awake listening to the low roar of traffic on
Third Avenue. It sounds, in the steadiness of its ebb
and flow, a little like the ocean. She is thinking about
her childhood holidays at the seaside when she hears
the dreadful, heart-stopping noise of metal crashing
into metal, glass breaking. A traffic accident. There is
a wheel-spinning silence, and then she hears someone
making the same sound the S-shaped editor had made
when the lights were switched off, someone in the
worst kind of panic, at the extremity of fear or pain, no
longer conscious of themselves. Cows make that noise
when giving birth and their calves become stuck,
Angel remembers. Angel grew up on a farm.

Once I Was Young, and So Unsure

Girlie learned to throw the discus in the paddock next to the shearing shed. She would bend her knees into a partial crouch, swing the arm holding the discus in wide arcs, then whirl around until momentum had built and she could send the discus spinning from her fingers. She retrieved it, picking her way through the thistles that grew there, and repeated what she had done, obsessively, until the light became too dim to see.

Although Girlie's classmates participated willingly in whatever the sports mistress cared to organize for them, they drew the line at the discus and shotput. They had all seen photographs and newsreel footage of the mannish Russian women athletes who were the stars of those events in the Melbourne Olympic Games. The images were invariably unflattering, and a message was successfully transmitted.

At fifteen Girlie was as heedful of codes of behaviour as any of her friends, but she was desperate to make the athletic team. The reason was a boy. She had fallen in love. Standing on the sideline at a school football game, Girlie had been the recipient of a glance from one of the visiting team's forwards. She started to breathe fast. Her palms became damp. It was her first big crush.

Girlie had never been kissed. She had held hands with a boy once, briefly, both of them looking the other way as if it wasn't happening. Now, when they saw each other, his ears turned red. She tried to imagine being kissed by the football player, but her mind went blank when she got to the part where his face bore down on hers. Like a horse at a water jump, she balked at any thought or expression of physical intimacy with the opposite sex. Her fright was compounded by the suspicion that she was as tall as the football player, if not taller.

She schemed to meet him. She found out that he was a long-distance runner and was sure to be at the athletics carnival where all the schools in the district competed against each other. She was a hockey player and a swimmer; athletics had never much interested her. What event could she enter where she would be sure to make the team? Girlie went to the sports mistress — her name was Miss Entwhistle — and requested some lessons in throwing the discus. She discovered that getting the discus to slice cleanly through the air had little to do with muscle and everything to do with balance and the way it left the hand.

She asked Miss Entwhistle if she might take a discus home to practise after school. And there, in the paddock next to the shearing shed, as her coordination improved, Girlie experienced the euphoria that comes with mastering a physical skill. She was good at exams, placing top of her class or close to it, but being a brain made her feel uncomfortable and apologetic, not like this, certain of herself, conquering. She was all of a piece, her body her own again. The tallness didn't matter so much, nor her small breasts, nor the still-horrifying monthly blood.

Not only that, but the underwater feeling of being in love vanished. It was as well because when she saw the boy again – she made the team with no trouble at all – he was walking arm-in-arm with another girl. She was small and busty. The two of them had the smug look of high school sweethearts who have been going together a long time and have already picked out names for their children.

Girlie was in fine form that day. The boys threw the discus first. When the teachers marking where the discuses landed saw the girls – there were only three of them – lining up, they had come in close, making jokes about it. Girlie will never forget the startled look on the teachers' faces when she sent the discus soaring over their heads. She threw so well she was picked to represent the district at the big state athletics carnival in Sydney.

They would be two nights in Sydney, billeted out with families. Miss Entwhistle was to be in charge of the girls on the train journey and on hand in Sydney if they needed her. Only one other of Girlie's classmates had made the team, a sprinter and high jumper who had hard, knotty calves and was very proud. She had no father, or at least there wasn't one living with her mother and herself, an irregular family arrangement that normally would have caused comment among her peers, adept as they were at imitating the censoriousness of their parents, but the athletic trophies lining her mantelpiece acted as garlic to vampires and warded off their spite.

Girlie sat on one side of Miss Entwhistle, the fatherless sprinter on the other. Members of the team from other towns boarded the train as they went along – the girls to Miss Entwhistle's compartment and the boys to one in the next carriage. The girls began to sing – *Ten Green Bottles, Dashing Away With a Smoothing Iron, The Road to Gundagai* – the usual stuff kids bellow on school trips to pass the time, or did back then, the more verses the better. One song in particular was very popular. It was about a ne'er-do-well who wooed and won a young woman but left her at the altar, whereupon she died:

> *He told her he loved her*
> *but oh how he lied*
> *oh how he lied*
> *oh how he lied.*
> *He told her he loved her*
> *but oh how he lied*
> *oh how he li-i-i-ied.*

They hammed the song up with tremolos. Some of the girls sang falsetto, others pretended to be baritones. Louder and louder they got, pink in the face and screechy, until Miss Entwhistle called for calm. They hadn't finished:

> *She went to heaven*
> *and flip-flop she flied*
> *flip-flop she flied*
> *flip-flop she flied*
> *she went to heaven*

and flip-flop she flied
flip-flop she fli-i-i-ied.

This last verse amused them all so much they fell into each other's laps giggling hysterically. Girlie had become as giddy as the rest of them. Her cheeks were burning, so she opened a window and put her head partway out. Miss Entwhistle pulled her back in, berating her for her lack of common sense. Someone told a story about a man who had his arm shorn off by a traffic sign when he stuck it out of a car window. It had happened only last week. A chastened Girlie affected an interest in watching the winter-green paddocks and rain-darkened haystacks slide by.

The families who were to billet the team were on the platform at Central Station. Miss Entwhistle called out names from a list. When Girlie's turn came, she found waiting for her not a family but a lone girl around her own age. They looked each other over. Girlie knew immediately, without having to think about it, that she shouldn't go with this girl. Her tunic was too short and belted too tight, her hair peroxided and teased, her ears pierced. Girlie was an A class student, Latin and French and all the rest of it; the girl standing opposite her was F class. F class students were either dull-witted, aboriginal, or wild. This girl was wild.

'My name's Marlene,' she said, and, guessing at Girlie's reluctance, grabbed her by the sleeve of her blazer and tugged her toward the ticket barrier. Girlie looked back. Her classmate, the sprinter, was standing in a circle with a family, the mother and father with their heads bent solicitously over her.

On the other side of the ticket barrier propped against a newspaper stand was Marlene's boyfriend. He was at least eighteen years old and had long ago left school. They went out the side entrance and into the night. The boyfriend's car – an FJ Holden – was a patchwork of unpainted duco. In the back was another youth.

Girlie should have turned around and gone to find Miss Entwhistle instead of climbing into the back seat of the car with that youth, but she lived in fear of appearing anything less than worldly-wise. It wasn't just that she was fifteen. Sad to say but many years were to pass before Girlie would be unafraid to act on her perceptions of people and situations.

As the car pulled out into George Street, Marlene slipped over and snuggled up to her boyfriend. Girlie watched stiff with apprehension. But she was also rehearsing what she would say to her friends, how she would describe the beat-up Holden, her new companions, the whizzing traffic, the city lights. She imagined their envy.

Marlene lived in Padstow, a drab working-class suburb in the eastern part of Sydney. There are no harbour views in Padstow, only fibro Housing Commission homes fronted by balding lawns. Marlene, the two youths, and poor Girlie, unable to give anything but monosyllabic answers to the desultory questions put to her, didn't go straight to Padstow. They went first to the beach at Maroubra.

It was around nine on a winter's evening; the car park at the beach was deserted. A lamp on the esplanade, its light weak and yellow, illuminated only haze. No sooner had Marlene's boyfriend stopped the car and put the handbrake on than he and Marlene jumped out, slamming the doors as they went, and disappeared down some steps to the beach.

Girlie and the youth sat in silence. The car windows fogged up. With his elbow, the youth rubbed a patch clear. They sat there a little longer. When he made his move, it was sudden, no inching across the seat or coy holding of hands. One minute he was staring out the window through the patch he had made, the next he was on top of her, his lips clamped hard on hers, his tongue filling her mouth, his hands busy at her breasts and then burrowing under her tunic. She was pinned by his weight. She thought she would suffocate.

Girlie was wearing full school uniform, a beret, blazer, sweater over a box-pleated serge tunic, long-sleeved blouse and tie. Under this, a petticoat, and under the petticoat, bloomers elasticized at the legs. These bloomers doubled as gym pants and were the same colour as the uniform and had stripes down the sides. Under the bloomers a suspender belt holding up thick stockings. And then sturdy cotton underpants.

These layers of clothing thwarted the youth. Making little grunting noises, he scrabbled away like a dog at the entrance to a rabbit warren. Girlie said over and over, numbly, her voice sounding to herself as if it were coming from a great distance, 'Stop, please. Stop, please.' He unzipped his pants and took her hand and placed it on his erect penis, curled her fingers around it.

At that moment, as Girlie's gorge rose, the car doors burst open letting in cold air and the boom of the ocean. Marlene leaned over the back seat and surveyed the situation. 'I thought he might try something like that,' she said, addressing Girlie.

'Bugger off, Marlene, or I'll stick this in you,' said the youth, shoving his penis back into his pants.

Marlene laughed, and her boyfriend backed the car out of the car park and into the street, tyres spurting gravel.

Marlene had no intention of spending any time with Girlie. She had billeted her only to have the days off school. They left the house at the same time in the morning, Girlie to catch the train to the sportsground and Marlene to her boyfriend's car, the engine idling, around the corner. Girlie threw her best distance yet in the discus event, but she was no competition for the professionally trained city kids.

As the train left the backyards and billboards of Sydney behind, Girlie could no longer keep the story of that first night to herself. She blurted out her tale to Miss Entwhistle. The sports mistress's face went stony. She was assessing whether she herself might be blamed in some way for Girlie's misadventure. Finally she said in a dismissive tone, 'So what's your problem? Nothing serious happened, did it?'

Girlie felt as foolish as Miss Entwhistle hoped she would. The fatherless sprinter, again sitting on the other side of the sports mistress, had overheard the exchange. Her mouth twitched into a small, knowing smile. Miss Entwhistle turned to the others. 'How about a song?'

...*flip-flop she fli-i-i-ied*.

I Experienced Again
a Terror of Possibilities

Anne-Marie is twenty-two years old. Anne-Marie is wailing. From past experience we know she will keep it up for hours, stockings around her ankles, buttons in the wrong buttonholes, mucus running unchecked out of her nose. She is inconsolable. Any effort to calm her is like throwing petrol on a fire. She gives vent to her misery and frustration the way a baby bawls, unflaggingly, until you can't help but marvel at her energy and wonder at the wellsprings of her dissatisfaction.

We inmates at Caritas have a high tolerance for disturbance. After all, all we have are our illnesses and their manifestations. Daily fracas with staff or each other, irrational outbursts, attempts to harm ourselves: this is our entertainment. More than that, it is proof we exist. The racket Anne-Marie makes, however, is too much even for us. When she starts up, we leave the dayroom, where we sit chain-smoking and staring dully about us, or stop our pacing near the nurses' station, and move out of earshot to the veranda or down to the occupational therapy building at the end of the garden.

. . .

I have the same diagnosis as Anne-Marie: chronic schizophrenia. But I am a beginner; this is my first hospitalization, Anne-Marie is my teacher, my exemplar. Anne-Marie has been hospitalized many times before. She has lost count of the number of shock treatments she has had. Anne-Marie is the real thing. I am not the real thing. I am pretending to be sick; I am making it up as I go along. The doctors believe my lies, and I am beginning to believe them myself. I want to be mad, and all I can say in my defence is that wanting to be mad is a madness in itself.

My troubles began when I walked out of my university exams. I had worked hard, crammed day and night, but when I read the first question of the first paper I couldn't make sense of it. I read it through again. Samuel Beckett might have written the question for all the meaning I could glean from it. When I sit for exams, I get overly anxious, but after I realized I wasn't going to be able to answer the question, I became quite peaceful.

I watched the other students scratching away, the dust motes created by the light coming through the high gothic windows, the hand of the clock jerking from minute mark to minute mark. A half hour into the three hour examination I stood up, pushing back my chair as I did so. The chair legs scraped on the wooden floor, and the sound reverberated through the examination hall. Nobody looked up as I walked down the aisle between the tables. It is easy, it only takes a moment, to derail a life.

I went home to my flat. Now that I was no longer on a scholarship, I would need money. I applied for and was given a job in a pub as a barmaid. I was an inept barmaid. I blushed furiously when addressed, and made countless blunders. The second day I dropped an unopened bottle of lemon squash syrup on the concrete floor behind the bar. It took an age to clean up the sticky liquid, the bits of glass. It was a wonder the publican didn't sack me then and there.

I started a romance with a barman who worked in the saloon bar. His name was Ray. He was married. He had spent two years in jail for car theft. A wrongful arrest, he claimed. He was no saint, he stressed when telling his story, but he didn't steal the car the police said he did. When Ray came to my place, he never bothered to use the toilet downstairs: he'd pee out the window. This is life, I told myself, grown-up life.

After closing on Christmas Eve, the publican and his wife threw a party for the staff, bottles of champagne and plates of prawns. I got drunk. I don't remember who put me to bed, but I woke up on the couch in the room where the publican's baby son slept. It must have been late in the morning because sunlight was streaming in, whitewashing the room with glare. The baby's nappy was overflowing with bright yellow shit, and he was standing up in his cot smearing the stuff on the wall. The smell was terrible. I started to cry.

I didn't go back to work. I had been crying for a week when a friend came by and said she thought I should see a psychiatrist. She had the name of one

already written on a piece of paper. This suggestion
did not displease me. I had long harboured an ambition to see a psychiatrist, viewing it as a daring and
sophisticated thing to do. It would mark me as an
interesting person.

How did I come to have such ideas? I can trace
my attraction to the world of madness to when I was
sixteen and read a novel by Janet Frame. It was called
The Edge of the Alphabet. Seduced by her language and
grim outlook, I memorized whole portions, reciting
them to myself as I went to sleep. *Now I, Thora Pattern
(who live at the edge of the alphabet, where words like plants
grow poisonous tall and hollow about the rusted knives and
empty drums of meaning, or, like people exposed to a deathly
weather, shed their fleshly confusion and show luminous,
knitted with force and permanence), now I walk day and
night among the leavings of people, places and moments.*
Living at the edge of the alphabet, that is to say, going
crazy, as I found out Janet Frame herself had done, was
an appealing notion, better than becoming a teacher or
marrying, or whatever else was expected of me.

The psychiatrist my friend recommended was
very handsome, patrician good looks, greying at the
temples, quite the lady-killer. I found out later his
first name was Paul, and so everybody referred to him
as Dr Paul, after the serial on the radio in the morning
by that name. You just had to mention he was your
doctor, and women would roll their eyes and hum the
theme song from the show.

Dr Paul asked me if I was depressed. I told him I
had been crying for a week. Did I hear voices? he
asked. I wasn't hearing voices, but I nodded yes. What
sort of voices? asked Dr Paul. Scolding voices, I
answered. You need a good, long rest, said Dr Paul,

and I couldn't have agreed with him more. You need to be cared for, he said, and I started to cry afresh.

•   •   •

Anne-Marie is wailing, and I am sitting on the veranda with Rhonda and Alfred, our legs up on the railing. Rhonda and Alfred are my buddies. We save places in the dining room for each other, and relay gossip. Rhonda is a working-class lesbian. When she walks, she rolls like a sailor; she swears like one, too. Fucking this, fucking that. She is in hospital because she tears strips off her own flesh when she is depressed. When she is really bad, she has to have her hands tied together. Alfred is as skinny as a bean and is always telling jokes. He is a postman. We don't know what he did to warrant being hospitalized, and that's what Rhonda and I are up to on the veranda, trying to wheedle it out of him. It has become a game with us. This time he gives in.

'Voices,' he finally decides to confide.

'Is that all? You told us you had done something terrible.'

'The voices ordered me to...' He stops.

'Come on, Alfred, tell us!'

'You know the inside of a biro, the plastic bit with ink in it?'

'Yes?'

'The voices ordered me to poke it down the hole in my penis.'

'Alfred, how disgusting!' we chorus.

Alfred feigns shame. He is enjoying the attention. 'They had to operate on me to get it out.'

•   •   •

Wanting attention myself, I play truant. I walk out the gates of the hospital while nobody is looking and into the nearest pub. One beer, two beers, I begin to feel good. The most desirable state is not to feel good but to feel nothing at all, and with that in mind I settle down in a corner by myself with a third beer, and a supply of coins for the jukebox. The afternoon becomes a jumble of faces and sound. Suddenly two male nurses from the hospital are bending over me and frog-marching me out of the bar.

It is dark outside. I consider running away, running wildly away, but the nurses have me firmly by each arm. They let me know in no uncertain terms how tedious they consider my behaviour. Walking up the steps of the entrance to the hospital, I stumble to emphasize my drunkenness, my unaccountability. The nurses pick me up and carry me over the threshold.

There is a fish tank, a big one, at least ten feet long, in the front hall of Caritas. The goldfish in the tank, with their dumb bulging eyes, have irritated me from the day I arrived. I break away from the nurses and run over to the tank and plunge my hand in. I come up with a rock from the bottom of the tank. I smash a hole in the glass with it. Water gushes out, along with the goldfish. Staff appear, try to rescue the fish, skid on the wet linoleum. The nurses slipping and sliding, lunging for the fish – I think it is the funniest sight I ever saw.

· · ·

In the matter of the goldfish, even Rhonda and Alfred think I went too far.

· · ·

There is a sign on the locker beside my bed: NO BREAKFAST. This means I am to have shock treatment. Since the day of the goldfish, I have had three shock treatments. I don't mind them. Being a shock-treatment patient makes me one of the elite around here. I have also come to look forward to the anaesthetic, that easy tipping into oblivion. I wake up a little groggy, with sticky patches at the temples where the doctor fastens the electrodes, but my normal self otherwise.

However after the last treatment I noticed I was forgetting things: the month of the year, what ward I was in. As much as I like my special status and the anaesthetic, I have become worried for my brain. I will go to the head sister and tell her I don't want any more shock treatments.

'I don't think you have any choice in the matter, Missie.'

I consider my options. I lock myself in a toilet stall, and refuse to come out. It works. It is decided I am one of the few on whom electroshock therapy has an adverse effect, causing me to become more aggressive rather than less. Instead I will be injected once a week with a sustained-release antipsychotic agent, fluphenazine hydrochloride.

· · ·

I sleep nearly all the time now. And I am hungry. No matter what I eat I am hungry.

· · ·

It is I who finds Anne-Marie. She is on the floor of the laundry room. She had gouged at the veins in her wrists with a piece of broken bottle until she hit an artery. The blood is spurting out of her as forcefully as the water escaping the fish tank. As I turn to go for help, I slip in her blood and fall.

. . .

'Anne-Marie had the right idea in getting shot of all this,' says Rhonda. She is trying to persuade a new patient, a middle-aged woman, to give up the bar of soap she is nibbling on. The woman thinks Rhonda is playing a game. She hides the soap behind her back. She is giggling. She is blowing bubbles.

. . .

Dr Paul says they have done everything they can for me and I can go home so long as I have my once-a-week fluphenazine injections. He summons my parents. They drive the four hundred miles to the city. I am called to Dr Paul's office, and there they are. My mother talks too much, too cheerily. My father is silent and sad. They don't know what to think, their clever daughter brought to this pass.

Dr Paul is in the most paternalistic, the most avuncular, of moods. She will be a good girl now, he tells my parents. My mother has gone shopping, bought me a dress. It is very short, as is the fashion. You have to be careful when you bend over. It is a lovely warm red colour.

. . .

We are home, in the pisé house with the corrugated iron roof shaded by pepper trees, the place I started from with my scholarship and dreams of glory. I remember back to the weeks before I left. My mother worked into the night to make me clothes on her sewing machine. She even made me an evening gown out of shantung silk. The world is your oyster, said my mother.

We eat mutton stew. Every two weeks or so, my father kills a sheep and hangs the sides of mutton on hooks in the meat house. My mother cuts the meat up with a saw. She puts her foot on the mutton to steady it, and then hacks away. She makes the stew but is hardly ever there to eat it. She is usually off playing bowls, winning pennants. She is crazy about bowls. While we eat my father listens to the stock prices on the radio. My father is dusty from his work on the tractor. We wash the stew down with black tea.

Every Thursday my mother and I drive across the flat plain to the doctor in Jerilderie. My mother chats to me about her days in the army as a young woman. She liked the war. She had a good time. It was the high point of her life.

The doctor is strange. He says, very heartily, Come in, young lady, and when I do step into his surgery, he says, very gruffly, I am not ready for you yet. I back out embarrassed. This happens every time we go to Jerilderie for my fluphenazine injection.

At the chemist in Jerilderie, I buy pancake makeup. The salesgirl shows me how to sponge it on. The makeup is bronze-coloured, and I have fair skin. Privately I think I look like a Red Indian, but the salesgirl tells me I am competition for Julie Christie. I also buy black eyeliner, and she teaches me how to ring my eyes with black.

The corrugated iron roof cracks in the heat. Through the fog of the fluphenazine I plan my career. I will be an actress, an artist, a writer. My father watches me. He grows sadder and sadder. You could mistake him for an undertaker his face is so long.

One day, while my mother is away playing bowls, he says, 'Pack your suitcase.' And I do. I put on my new dress, which barely fits me now, so much mutton stew have I eaten, and carefully apply the pancake makeup and the eyeliner.

My father is waiting for me in his utility. We drive to the railway station at Narrandera. There are flocks of galahs by the road, pecking up spilled wheat. At the station he hands me my ticket and five hundred dollars. 'You have to get away from here. No more injections. Go back to Sydney. Start over again.' He kisses me good-bye. He is crying. I am not crying. I am too frightened to cry.

· · ·

I am hungry as usual. I want to go to the buffet car and have a toasted ham-and-cheese sandwich. But I don't move. I am certain everybody on the train knows my story. They will stare at me, point and laugh. Shame keeps me in my seat as if stuck there by glue. The hours go by, and I don't move. Then I feel the small ache that means I am menstruating. I should get up and go to the toilet. But I can't. I feel dampness between my legs. It spreads. Still I can't make myself move. I am on my way to Sydney to begin my life again.

MAPPING MYSELF

The day after I arrived in New York, it began to snow. It snowed hard for three days. The sky sagged and fell in, a vast tent whose poles had been kicked out and the guy ropes cut. It doesn't snow in the country I come from, at least not where people live, so I watched fascinated as New Yorkers – who would believe this? – skied in the streets and cars became mounds of snow. Long as boats the cars were, or so they seemed compared with the ones back home. Most of all, from those first few days, I remember the quiet. The muffled quiet of a big city covered with snow. For me, even after it stopped snowing, it stayed quiet, the sound somehow switched off, and I was as lonely as I'd ever been before and never want to be again.

It would be better for my story if I could tell you I knew no-one in New York, that's how lonely I was, but the truth of the matter is I did know someone:

Angela, a lesbian friend from home. She had moved to New York to live with an American named Frieda. A large-boned woman, Frieda had a way about her of filling a room. In Angela, who had the cunning of a courtier, she had chosen well, an Alice to her Gertrude. Both were by way of being professional feminists and had met in Mexico City in 1975 at the International Women's Year conference. Angela's friends back home were exceedingly envious of her alliance with Frieda. She had made a good marriage, so to speak.

You might have noticed this yourself, but people who have the ability to fill a room with their presence usually work at it. They have tricks. One of Frieda's tricks was whispering. She was always lowering her voice so you had to lean forward to hear her. Not wanting to miss out on whatever it was that was making you listen so carefully, someone else would lean forward, too. Pretty soon everyone in the vicinity found themselves straining toward Frieda. This had the general effect of making her the centre of attention. Her words sounded wiser than they actually were.

So it was that after I had been sleeping on Frieda and Angela's couch for two weeks, Frieda took me aside and said, sotto voce, 'You have to leave.'

'What's that?' I said, cocking my head.

'You have to leave. Angela's too embarrassed to tell you herself.'

'Oh.' Even now I prickle with shame at having been so obtuse as to overstay my welcome. The next day I moved into the Martha Washington Hotel for Women.

Although I was fearful about my future, I wasn't

unhappy to be kicked out of Frieda and Angela's. I was at a crossroads in more ways than one, increasingly dissatisfied with my way of life. Back home my friends were much like Frieda and Angela, feminists of one sort or another, and while I loved my friends dearly, I had become tired of the righteous indignation, the beleaguered whining, the easy dismissal of just about everything you could name. I had come away to experience a different world, I'd hoped. But on my first night in New York, as a kindness but also to impress, Frieda and Angela had taken me to a party filled with feminist luminaries: Kate Millett, Robin Morgan, Rita Mae Brown, I forget who else. I have a souvenir of that night, a polaroid of me with Kate Millett, our eyes ruby-red from the flash.

Well, I was impressed. These women were formidable: so sure of themselves. I flickered uncertainly in comparison. Nonetheless, their conversations were remarkably similar to the ones my friends and I had back home. The gambits they used in flirting with one another were identical, and the music to which they listened. *You and I travel to the beat of a different drum...* This is not why I had come to New York, I can remember thinking.

I would describe my life up until then as improvised. We feminists were mapping ourselves, but it was an awkward process, lacking often in dignity, or so it seemed to me. I might have been dissatisfied with my way of life, but what other kinds were there? I had grown up in a country town, gone to university, and plunged into a world of left-wing politics and marginal artistic types, where I'd stayed put. At the Martha Washington, I was finally out on my own.

Run by two Moroccans named Abdul and Latif,

the Martha Washington Hotel was an education, as
they say. It was one step above a welfare hotel, with a
clientele made up primarily of women stranded in
New York by circumstance and lacking the where-
withal to leave. Abdul and Latif shamelessly bullied
their guests, some of whom had been there for as long
as twenty or thirty years. Occasionally, in the hallways, faded Southern belles fought with their Yankee
counterparts. They'd go at it like feuding wives in a
harem, kicking, biting, scratching, until Abdul and
Latif came running to pull them apart.

The rooms were spartan: a narrow bed, an arm-
chair, a table tarted up with gold paint, and a lamp.
Every floor had a communal bathroom. At first it was
hard to get a fix on the other women. I'd glimpse
someone out of the corner of my eye, but before I could
take a good look, they would scuttle away like crabs
and be gone. As the weeks went by, some of the
women on my floor became better known to me. Latif,
the nicer of the two Moroccans, would fill me in on
their histories, sad ones for the most part, because
somewhere along the line – why else would anyone put
up with Abdul, Latif, and a dank-smelling room at the
Martha Washington Hotel unless this were so? – they
had been engulfed by life and lost their reason.

Mrs Van Allen, next door to me, was one such
unfortunate. According to Latif, she came from a social
register family and had pots of money. An avid show
jumper in her youth, she'd become unhinged when her
favourite horse died. ('Goodness!' I'd said when Latif
told me this.) Mrs Van Allen had vigorous grey hairs
growing out of her nostrils and ears, and always wore a
wool coat buttoned up to the neck, a misshapen felt
hat, and elastic-sided riding boots. She carried assorted

rubbish around with her in plastic shopping bags, along with a bundle of bank books bound together with a rubber band, as I had noticed one day. And she was always in a tearing hurry, looking at her watch and muttering to herself, like the White Rabbit. One time she must have been going somewhere special because she had polished her boots and arranged an immense turban on her head. The turban was made from strips of bed sheet. Dirty bed sheet.

I tried hard in my months at the Martha Washington to figure out the kind of life I wished for myself, the person I would be. One day I came upon a set of blue-and-white dishes in the window of Azuma, cheap stuff from Taiwan, but I wanted it: sugar bowl, creamer, gravy boat, the works, and a table to put it on and a house to go around it, I suppose, although I dared not let my fantasies go too far in that direction. I knew a woman once, her name was Nancy, a concert pianist married to a violinist. Somehow she and her husband became involved with a tyrannical Trotskyite group that forbade its members to partake of bourgeois pleasures of any description. Apparently Nancy succumbed to an impulse to buy just such a dinner set. She was expelled by the group, and her husband divorced her. The last time I saw Nancy, she was driving a bus and had a beaten-down air about her.

There was no need for me to be expelled by a no-consequence Trotskyite group; I was already on the outer with the whole human race. After a bit the blue-and-white dishes were taken out of the Azuma window, but by then I had discovered the sixth floor of Bloomingdale's, where the displays of tableware are laid out in a circle. If you browse counterclockwise, fine china comes first, then cutlery and silver-plate, followed by glass and cut-crystal. I spent hour upon hour there, finding solace among the chafing dishes, salt-and-pepper cellars, ice buckets, and caviar bowls. If nobody was looking, I'd maybe pick up a cup or plate and hold the cold surface against my cheek.

The staff on the sixth floor were a nonchalant crew. They passed the time of day yawning or shooting the air-conditioned breeze with each other while customers vainly asked for assistance. I made friends with one of them, a Mrs Gluck, who was happy to weigh the merits of Spode versus Minton or Limoges versus Villeroy & Boch once she had overcome her initial distrust. I remember Mrs Gluck asking me what I liked best among this wealth of stylish objects. After lengthy deliberation, I chose a Wedgwood set, white with a raised pattern of strawberries and vine leaves. The cups were particularly satisfactory, being high-sided. Not coincidentally, my grandmother had one like it, only hers was green.

The weeks went by and the weather warmed up. Abdul and Latif unbuttoned their shirts to the navel, but Mrs Van Allen kept her coat on. I worried about her in the heat in that outfit until I realized she was so uncomfortable inside her skin that a little prickly wool on the outside meant nothing. By then I had a routine. I started my days with breakfast in a greasy spoon, having worked out that was the meal where you got the most for your money. Then I'd find a café where I could nurse a cup of coffee and read the papers. After that, the movies, a museum, bookshops, Bloomingdale's. In the evenings, although I tried not to do this too often, I might go to a bar. Usually I only had to pay for the first drink, and then somebody would come over and start buying them for me. What the hell, it was company.

One night in a place where the mirrors were mottled with foxing and the bar had so many coats of varnish it was soft to the touch, I struck up a conversation with a tubby chap, a set-changer on Broadway. He was nice enough. Drink as I might that evening, and one of the reasons I favoured this bar was the extra-large gin-and-tonics they served, I couldn't make the gnawing feeling that everything had gone wrong go away. I left the bar rather abruptly. My drinking companion followed me out into the street.

'I'm coming home with you,' he said.

'No, you're not.'

'Yes, I am.' He began to tug at my sleeve.

'Go away.' But he wouldn't. He kept tugging. So I hauled off and hit him. He stood there on the pavement, for the moment stunned. And then he turned into Rumpelstiltskin. His face went red. His cheeks puffed out. He balled his hands into fists and stamped his foot. 'Lady,' he screamed. 'You're crazy.' It occurred to me he was right.

Sentimental Journey

William – husband of Lotte, his third marriage, her first, of East Seventy-second Street in New York, an industrial designer well liked by all who know him, mentor to many a young person getting a start in the business, befriender of doormen, shop assistants, bus drivers, transit cops, security guards, a smile and a kind word for everybody who crosses his path, big-hearted sometimes to a fault, or so Lotte thinks – was deliberating one morning on what to wear, he being particular about his clothes. Holding up a navy-blue tie with small white polka dots against a grey suit, he said to Lotte, 'I once gave Veronica a dress. It was blue with white polka dots just like this tie.'

Veronica was William's stepmother.

'It was a sweet dress,' continued William. 'Little white cuffs, white collar. I bought it for thirty-nine dollars at the May Company.'

'Did she like it?' asked Lotte.

William looked stricken. His face lost its colour. He closed his eyes. Lotte went over to him.

He opened his eyes. 'No, she wasn't crazy about that dress. In fact, she hated it.'

William and Lotte hadn't been married long enough for them to know every last thing about each other. Over breakfast, at her urging, he told her the story of the blue dress with white polka dots. It made him late for his first appointment.

William was born in New Orleans. His father was a salesman for United Fruit. His name was Walter, but he went by the nickname of Gee Whiz Walter, or just plain Gee Whiz, because as a kid he was always getting up to the kind of caper that elicited the response, 'Gee Whiz, Walter.'

William's mother was called Dolores. She was from Cuba and had long eyelashes that curled at the ends. Dolores's father, a translator for Teddy Roosevelt and his Rough Riders during the Spanish-American War, had been forced to leave his native country because of his Yankee sympathies. Dolores, made of stronger stuff than her eyelashes would have anyone think, always took pains to refer to that war as the Cuban War of Independence.

Gee Whiz had thick brown wavy hair and a gentle smile. Unfortunately, to use William's terminology, he was a player. A ladies' man. He married Dolores only because she was pregnant with William. His folks came from Alabama. They were people of prejudice, members of the Ku Klux Klan, and couldn't find it within themselves to welcome a young Cuban woman into the bosom of the family. That and Gee Whiz's philandering – the final straw was a pass he made at Lilly, Dolores's best friend – caused their marriage to founder. Gee Whiz took off for parts unknown, promising Dolores he would contribute $30 a month toward the raising of his son. He posted money the first month but was seldom heard from after that.

William grew up surrounded by women. As well as his mother, there was Dolores's sister, Maria, the aforementioned Lilly, and Granma Todd, Lilly's mother. All this Lotte knew already. The part she didn't know, the one involving the polka-dot dress, occurred when William was eleven years old. Dolores received a letter from Gee Whiz asking if William could come and spend the summer holidays with him. He had settled down in Los Angeles and was doing well. Very well, in fact, as he was now an executive for the Zellerbach Paper Company. He had married again, to Veronica, an Oklahoman. Veronica was looking forward to making William's acquaintance. He enclosed the train fare.

Gee Whiz's failure to pay child support rankled in Dolores about as deep as those things do with women left by husbands to make ends meet, but she couldn't say no to this request. Every boy needs to know his father. So it was, at the beginning of the summer of 1935, that William, Dolores, Aunt Maria, Lilly, and Granma Todd set out for the New Orleans railway station. They were driven there by Louis, Maria's beau, in Louis's Studebaker. Louis was a manager for the General Shoe Company of St Louis.

'I have a vivid memory of Uncle Louis,' said William. Lotte was pouring the tea. He was waiting for the English muffins to brown in the toaster. 'He was very tall, about six foot three. And he had a slight paunch. He was always well-shaven, spotlessly clean. I never saw him in anything else but a white suit, black shoes, black silk stockings, black tie, and a panama hat. On occasion, a blue tie.'

William sat in the front seat of the Studebaker on the way to the station. Louis always let him sit there. He felt that women sat in the back and the men in the front. Louis tried to be a father to William. He used to take him to his office on Saturday mornings while he finished up his paperwork for the week. Then he would get a shoeshine downstairs while William watched. Later the women would join them for lunch at Thompson's Cafeteria. Louis let William have any dessert he wanted.

'You call him Uncle Louis. Did he marry Maria?' asked Lotte.

'Later on. They were waiting for the divorce to come through from her husband Charlie. Charlie also was a player.'

'The women in your family had lousy luck when it came to men,' said Lotte. Not only were there Gee Whiz and Charlie, but Dolores's father, having brought his family to the United States, promptly deserted them. Dolores's mother died shortly thereafter. Dolores said she died of anger.

'You have to remember there was a lot of pressure on men to propose to women in those days,' said William. 'It wasn't enough just to be sweethearts. And New Orleans, because of the gambling and prostitution, attracted the players. Salesmen, other transients. Salesmen always had the cover of going on a trip. But Louis, he was okay.' A pause while William reviewed what he knew of Louis from an adult perspective. 'At least I think he was.'

The New Orleans railway station was glass-covered and cavernous. The women climbed in and out of the train to inspect William's seat. He had a fold-down berth. Granma Todd's husband, long deceased, had been a Mississippi steamboat captain and the possessor of a leather suitcase with brass fittings. This had been produced, the leather oiled and the fittings polished, for William to take to Los Angeles. It was very heavy. Now it was lifted into place in William's compartment.

'Oh, I forgot. Jimmy came to the railway station that day. There were more men than usual around,' said William.

'Who was Jimmy?'

'Lilly's friend. He and Lilly married later on too, but at that time he was married to somebody else. Lilly was his mistress.' William over-enunciated the word 'mistress' the way an eleven-year-old boy trying to be nonchalant might.

Lotte was highly amused by this piece of information. She laughed so much she started to cough. 'Sounds like they were all players.'

'Lilly had a lot of guys,' admitted William.

Louis and Jimmy went off to check out the porters. They came back with a black man who was even taller than Louis.

'His name was Henry Collins. He was very gracious. He looked like the porters you see in the old movies,' said William, by now sitting down and buttering the muffins.

'You remember his name after all this time?'

'You bet I do. We spent the next three days and nights together.'

Louis gave Henry Collins a twenty-dollar tip, a

large sum of money in those days. He let every-body know he was giving the porter this vast amount.

'You take care of my boy or your life is not worth shit,' said Louis to Henry Collins.

'He talked that way,' said William.

'Louis, Louis,' chorused the women.

There was William, still in knickers, on the Sunset Limited, setting out on his first journey away from home. As they went along, he could see cowboys on their horses out the window, who waved at the train. William waved back.

The first stop was San Antonio, where the train changed lines. The wait while they took on coal and passengers was long, so William ventured onto the platform. He couldn't believe how high the sky was. He could hear the sound of cattle – destined for the slaughterhouses in Chicago – in the stockyards nearby, so he wandered in the direction of their bellowing. Unable to find any cattle, he turned around and came back. The train was gone.

William was a punchy kid, not easily frightened, but when he saw that train gone, he stood there mouth drying, legs rooted to the ground. A porter came by. William told him what had happened. Together they hurried to find the station master, who phoned the next station down the line and asked them to flag the train. Then they piled into a car and went in chase.

From the speeding car, William could see the train puffing across the flat countryside toward the little station. It came to a halt. When they arrived, Henry Collins was standing by the train all alone. He opened his arms and William ran into them. 'Boy, you never get off this train again. You stay in my pocket,' he said. William felt good to be in those strong arms, to be swung by them up into the train.

When the train pulled into Los Angeles two and a half days later, Gee Whiz was standing on the platform exactly where the Pullman bearing William stopped. He was nervous but obviously pleased to see his son. Veronica was waiting at home for them, he told William. But when they reached the apartment on Wilshire Boulevard, Veronica wasn't there. Gee Whiz got more and more nervous. He showed William everything in the house twice. Still she didn't come home. He suggested they go for a walk in Westlake Park. They ran into her on their way back.

Veronica had black hair with an iridescent sheen to it and a sharp nose and pointed chin. Those features combined with her sallow skin made William from that first meeting on always think of her as a hen, a sleek black hen.

'Her skin was yellow like a chicken's beak,' elaborated William, in case Lotte hadn't fully understood why he should have formed that mental image.

At first Veronica was civil to William, but her dislike of him soon became apparent. Plain and simple, she was jealous, as stepmothers sometimes are of offspring from former marriages. Lotte could sympathize with Veronica. She herself has had twinges of jealousy toward William's two sons from his first marriage, who are grown men gone their own way. But William, being only eleven, couldn't fathom Veronica's hostility. All he knew was she didn't like him.

'I was something she'd rather step on than stoop down to kiss,' said William.

William was a good boy. Dolores kept a strict

ship. He always folded his clothes, lined his towel up on the rack, and tucked his bed in the way a marine would. He was neat in appearance, his shoes shined, his belt cinched tight around his waist. And he was quick to offer to help about the house. Veronica had nothing to complain about. This annoyed her more than anything else.

William began to spend all his time outside the house. He went on long walks down Wilshire Boulevard. He discovered the Cord motor car show-room. The salesmen let him sit in the front seat of the display models. He was even allowed to dry the cars off after they had been washed.

'Cord motor cars. What did they look like?' Lotte is of another generation.

William made space among the breakfast things to draw one. 'If you saw a Cord on the street today, it wouldn't be dated. They had a wraparound grille like this...' he drew a front-on view, '...that said speed.' Then he drew the car from the side. 'Elaborate chrome exhaust pipes. Fenders hiding the wheels. And a racing slant to its windscreen.'

The Cord's most singular feature was its auto-matic transmission, the first ever. It was operated by a little knob on the end of a stick on the steering column. William drew this too. 'Vroom, vroom, vroom,' went William, and moved an imaginary knob back and forth.

William started going even further afield, down by the May Company and the Brown Derby. He would come home and describe to Veronica the movie stars he'd seen coming in and out of that famous restaurant. Veronica would tell him he was making it all up. He couldn't have walked that far, she argued.

Gee Whiz was working long hours at the Zellerbach Paper Company, but even when he did have time to spend with William, he never overcame his initial nervousness. William felt very alone. He began to go out by himself at night as well. One evening he went to see a Frankenstein movie. Coming back through the park, a man tried to grab hold of him. His breath smelled of alcohol. William kicked him in the leg and ran all the way home. He burst into the apartment panting hard. Gee Whiz wanted to know what had happened. William told him.

'Don't pay him no heed. He's lying. He always lies,' said Veronica. Repeating these words for Lotte, William was stricken all over again.

Perhaps because of this incident, Gee Whiz found a job for William at the Zellerbach Paper Company. For two months William cleaned out the storage bins in Zellerbach Paper's warehouse. It was filthy work. He had to tie a handkerchief over his nose and mouth to stop the dust choking him. All he was given to assist him in this task was a pan and broom and some rags.

William drove to work with Gee Whiz in his Plymouth. He sat up front on the way there, but on the return journey Gee Whiz made him sit in the back with newspapers underneath him. William looking like Al Jolson in blackface finally gave Veronica something to complain about. It was decreed that he couldn't come in the apartment until he hosed himself down in the backyard. William found all of this humiliating.

He sent some of the money he earned home to Dolores. What he had over after he bought his lunch he saved. He had a plan. He had seen a dress in the window of the May Company that he thought might suit Veronica. It was blue with white polka dots and had a white collar and cuffs. He imagined Veronica wearing this dress to church and the minister commenting on it, as had happened to Granma Todd when she wore the floral one he'd selected for her.

He told his father about the plan. His father was delighted. After work on William's last day at the Zellerbach Paper Company, the two of them went to the May Company store. William knew what floor the dress could be bought on, what size Veronica was. Gee Whiz was surprised that his son was so knowledgeable about women's clothing.

Gee Whiz put the box containing the dress on Veronica's side of the bed. When William was cleaned up, Gee Whiz told her there was a present waiting for her in the bedroom. Her eyes became saucers when she saw the box was from the May Company. William stood by anticipating the first hug he would get from Veronica, his need for her to like him hurting him like a sliver of wood jammed under a fingernail. She was holding the dress up against herself and surveying her image in the mirror, over the moon in her pleasure at the gift, when Gee Whiz told her William had bought the dress for her.

Veronica's face registered complete dismay. With a sleeve in one hand and a shoulder in the other, she tugged. The dress ripped. Gee Whiz sank to his knees. Veronica left the room. Later William could hear them arguing.

William stared out the window at the water tank on the building opposite. He looked to Lotte as if he were casting around for a moral to his story. He must have failed to come up with one because the next thing

he said was, 'I was good at buying women's clothes.'
And he stretched his neck as if to preen.

OLIVE TREES, A CAPER BUSH, AND HEDGES OF LAVENDER

Dirt lay in drifts on the floor of the hotel room. Lotte got out a dictionary, fumbled through its pages. She found the word she needed. 'Sporco, sporco,' she said to the porter and pointed at the floor. The porter looked blank. She mimed sweeping the floor. The porter, she was certain, was stifling a desire to laugh at her. It wasn't that he was avoiding being rude. Rather that laughter, even the derisive kind, was incompatible with the surly indifference he was intent on projecting.

'Ah, sporco,' he finally let himself say. He fetched a broom, shifted the dirt from one side of the room to the other, and then waited for Lotte to make a fuss, not quite catching her eye, his shoulders ready to shrug away complaints. Lotte, tired from her journey, let him go.

She opened the shutters. A wind banged them

shut again. She worked the bolt loose on the door of the balcony. Ordinarily, to have a balcony like this one, jutting out over the ocean and a grandstand view of the famous volcano across the strait, steep-sided with smoke curling out the top the way a child might draw one, would be a pleasure; but the detritus of winter was here, too, upholstering ledges, banked into corners. She up-ended a faded canvas chair, spilling a pile of wet leaves and other less identifiable matter onto the floor, and sat down to warm herself in the mild spring sunshine.

The sunshine faded. Spring in this part of the world, she was discovering, meant sudden, pummeling rain. The sea below started to toss. The poplar trees surrounding the church on the promontory opposite the hotel strained into arcs. I'm tired, she thought; a nap, things will seem better after a nap. The pillowcases and sheets were damp. The bed had been made up at the end of last summer.

Eyes shut, a pin jabbed in a map, that's how she had found this place: an archipelago, islands scattered across the sea like knucklebones in a game of jacks. She remembered some photographs she had seen in a travel magazine, cube-shaped white-washed houses, precipitous cliffs, a midnight-blue sea.

'Yes, yes,' said the man to whom Lotte spoke when she called long-distance from New York to see if the hotel was open.

'Your name?' she asked.

'Romeo.' The stress on the middle syllable. Rohmay-oh.

'I'll be arriving April third,' she told him.

'Yes, yes,' said Romeo.

Later she realized she hadn't told him how long

she would be staying so she called back. A woman answered the phone.

'Can I speak to Romeo?' Lotte requested.

'Who?'

'Romeo. He speaks English.'

'Romeo doesn't speak English.'

A moment of confusion, and then Lotte realized that Romeo might not speak English but the woman she was talking to did. Again she made a reservation and this time included the length of her stay.

'Yes, yes,' said the woman.

Greedy for the extra lire, or lacking the English to explain it, they neglected to inform her that spring was still off-season on the island. It was the time when they readied the hotel for the summer. When she arrived she found the public spaces of the hotel littered with piles of lumber, bags of concrete, mounds of sand. In addition, the kitchen was in the process of being enlarged. To eat at the hotel was impossible, and no other restaurants on the island had opened yet either.

The rain stopped. Lotte went for a walk. The whole town was preparing for the summer season. Small three-wheeled trucks, loaded up with building materials and crates of mineral water, tore through the narrow streets, forcing her into alcoves hollowed into the walls for the safety of pedestrians. She called in at the ferry office near the wharf and asked the man at the desk if he could recommend another hotel. His brother had a hotel, he informed her, but unfortunately it was closed. All the hotels were closed except the one at which she was staying.

She went up to the church on the promontory and rattled its locked doors and then took the road that looped around the back of the town past the cemetery and a building angled against a rocky escarpment. Lotte had already admired this building, with its honeycomb of rooms and stepped terraces, from the ferry as they approached the island. It was too big for a private house, and yet no signs advertised it as a hotel. She sniffed the air. Somewhere close there were orange trees in blossom.

Lotte heard the fish seller's cry before she saw him. Women came out and hung over the walls. The fish seller shovelled finger-sized fish from his barrow onto a scale, tipped them into plastic bags. No-one so much as glanced at Lotte. Back near the wharf, she passed a tall man, of a big build but bent over, with shoulder-length hair in a pony tail. He gave no sign of seeing her either, but he had gone about ten paces when he turned on his heel and caught up with her.

'You look worried. Can I be of assistance?' His English was accented, his tone peremptory. He had a frown scored in wavy lines across his forehead. Lotte put his age at around sixty. Figuring she had nothing to lose, she told him about her hotel, the damp, dirty room.

'Bah. Those fascists! Terrible hotel! Here, come and have a glass of juice with me.' He pointed through a gate to a courtyard where there was a table and some chairs. Lotte nodded her assent.

He fetched the juice from inside the house and then introduced himself. His name was Cosmo. He had lived on the island for thirty years.

He started to tell her his country of origin but interrupted himself. It was so long ago it didn't matter. And her name? Where was she from? How many days did she intend to stay? His eyes never left her face. He was making up his mind about something.

The juice was bitter and dark red in colour.

'What's this?' asked Lotte, holding up her glass.

'Blood oranges,' said Cosmo. 'You want sugar?'
Lotte shook her head.

When they had finished the juice, he said, 'You have noticed the pink building behind the town? That's mine. My hotel. You can stay there. As my guest. I can't accept money because we are not open.'

She hesitated. It had to be better than where she was now. 'I'd like that. If it is not too much trouble.'

'The staff all sleep here, so you'd be by yourself. With no telephone. The rooms don't have them.'

'I'll be fine.'

'You can have your meals with us if you like.'

'You're very kind.'

A good-looking youth with a dark tan, gleaming teeth, and black hair shaved close to the skull came into the courtyard, and Cosmo introduced him to Lotte – his name was Felix – and asked him to take her up to the hotel. Cosmo himself had work to which he had to attend. He would come by later and see if she needed anything.

Felix waited outside her old hotel while Lotte collected her bag and told the management she was leaving. They seemed relieved. She and Felix, who was shy about speaking English, walked along in companionable silence. In the driveway of Cosmo's hotel, they passed a man hoeing weeds. Lotte could see two women on one of the terraces shaking the dust out of blankets.

Entered by double doors from a large terrace, Lotte's room was painted white and sparsely furnished.

A second door at the side opened onto a smaller terrace shaded by an olive tree. Tiny windows near the ceiling let in air and light. Felix went off and came back with two old-fashioned deckchairs, the sort that are made from varnished wood and have brass hinges. He set them up on the terrace for her. While he was doing this, Lotte checked the sheets on the bed. They smelled of soap and sun.

Felix made to leave. Lotte had a tip ready. She offered it to him.

'No, no, no!' he said, laughing and pushing away her hand, clearly embarrassed, and ran off down the steps. Lotte was momentarily puzzled by this. And amused. It was not often a hotel employee turned down a tip. She unpacked her bag and then went to sit out on the terrace. The air was gauzy up here. It was isolated, but splendidly so, with the village spread out below and the volcano across the strait smoking contentedly. She would spend the next week walking and reading. She had lucked out.

Lotte had dozed off when she heard footsteps and a cough. It was Cosmo wanting to show her around the hotel garden. As she quickly found out, he was inordinately proud of this garden and especially of its dry-stone walls.

'I built the walls with my own hands,' he said, working his satisfaction with himself like a child sucking on hard candy. They came to an olive tree, an old one with a gnarled trunk. A wall had been cleverly built around it. Cosmo stopped to caress the fissured bark.

'Beautiful, eh?' He directed her attention to a small meadow nearby filled with wild fennel in flower, and then to the red poppies that had seeded at random here and there. 'See all that? It is hard to explain to the gardeners that they must leave the weeds. They want to pull them up, make everything neat and tidy. It is wild on purpose. That is my plan.'

'Paradise gardening,' said Lotte, who wasn't particularly interested in gardening herself but knew a little about it because one of her clients was a writer of hugely popular gardening books. Lotte was a literary agent.

'Paradise gardening, huh? That's what you call it in America?' said Cosmo. He turned to the hotel itself. 'Now look closely at that pillar. See how nothing is straight, everything is sloping. That is my plan too. I studied Babylonian architecture. Sumerian architecture.'

'It's very beautiful. The whole village is beautiful.'

'That is because of me,' said Cosmo. 'The islanders didn't care. They had no pride of place. They lived in the streets, the bars, on their fishing boats. I made them accept a building code. Otherwise this place would look a mess like the rest of the Mediterranean. Notice also how there are no poles for electricity and the telephone. All the wires go under the ground. That is my plan too. There are no street lamps either. You've seen the street lamps down this way. Ugly things made from – how do you say it? – a metal, shiny.'

'Aluminum,' supplied Lotte.

'Yes. Aluminum. The Mafia are in on it. They own the company that makes the poles and they force the communes – the municipal councils – into buying them. You don't need street lights in a place this small. You can use a torch if it's dark.'

Lotte looked across at him. He must have been a handsome man once. She was beginning to get his measure. A human bulldozer but likeable all the same because every now and again he paid attention. He took stuff in, which is more than many men of his age and temperament did.

They came to a path bordered by a low hedge of lavender. Across the way was an orchard where the orange trees she had smelled on her first foray were in blossom. Lotte sniffed the air again, getting her fill of the sharp scent.

Cosmo listed what he could harvest in his orchard. 'Figs. Almonds. Pomegranates. Quinces. I think that's what you say in English. Oranges. They have their blossoms. And lemons. They are blossoming. The lemons from those trees! They are as big as this.' And he made a shape the size of a football with his hands.

Agapanthus in pots, geraniums of the purest red, more hedges, of lavender and also of rosemary and oleander, an agave at least ten foot tall and as wide, a hundred-year-old caper bush, all were pointed out by Cosmo, admired by Lotte. Cosmo went his way after telling her they sat down for dinner at eight.

Lotte read for a while, Norman Lewis's *Naples 44*. The hotel was very quiet; the man working in the garden and the two women fixing up rooms had gone home. Around seven-thirty she set off for the waterfront.

Halfway down she passed a woman trailed by a tired child. The child tripped and started to bawl. Lotte picked him up and brushed him down. The woman – obviously the child's mother – thanked her. She was English. Lotte remarked on it, and they chatted briefly. Her name was Helen. She had come to the island as part of a gastronomic tour of the Mediterranean, and had met and married the baker's son.

'You never know what's in store, do you? The baker's son!' said Lotte's new acquaintance. She laughed at this as if it were the biggest joke under the sun, opening her mouth wide so you could see her back teeth. Underneath the laughter, she was sad. When she stopped laughing, she asked Lotte where she was staying. Lotte told her.

Helen's face darkened. 'With Cosmo? He's mad, you know.'

Lotte didn't know what to say. 'He's got a forceful personality, that's for sure. But he's okay.'

'No, no. He's quite mad. So be careful,' said Helen, and took her child by the hand and disappeared into the dusk.

They sat at a long table in a room decorated with amphorae that Cosmo had retrieved on diving expeditions in the waters around the island. Cosmo was at the top of the table, Lotte to his right, Felix to the left. The staff all resembled Felix in that they were glossily young and had deep tans and gleaming teeth. A fire had been set in the fireplace because the evening was chilly.

The conversation was animated and multilingual, Cosmo orchestrating the proceedings and translating for Lotte when necessary. They talked sport and politics, teased one another, and sniped at the islanders. The islanders, in Cosmo's book, were either fascists or simpletons or both. He had numerous feuds going with them.

One feud, which Lotte pieced together from

comments here and there, involved the hotel she had checked into first. Cosmo had opened an outdoor disco on the waterfront directly under this hotel. The music kept their guests awake. Cosmo refused to have his band turn down its amplifiers. The management of the hotel decided that if they couldn't beat him they'd join him, and built a dance floor overlooking the disco so their guests could also shimmy the night away to the music of Cosmo's band. Cosmo was enraged. He built a high wall between his disco and their hotel. Now it was the other side's turn to retaliate. Cosmo and his staff spent part of the dinner predicting what that might involve.

The feud with the hotel was one of long standing, and the episode of the disco only the latest instalment. Lotte wondered how Cosmo could live all these years at war with his neighbours. Island life would get claustrophobic enough without everybody hating each other. She watched him. His lip curled whenever the subject of the islanders came up. He was a man streaked with bitterness.

They ate ravioli followed by squid. The squid had sand in it. Lotte left most of it on her plate.

'What's the matter? Don't you like it?' demanded Cosmo.

'It tastes good, but I'm not very hungry,' said Lotte diplomatically.

'Go on, eat it up. It's fresh from the sea out there. You must eat it.'

'No, truly, I've had enough.'

'Come on now.'

'No, I can't eat it.' He was about to insist again, but Lotte folded her napkin and put it by her plate. He got the message.

Canned peaches for dessert, and then the staff went their separate ways. Cosmo and Lotte settled down in front of the fire, each with a brandy.

'You like my staff?' he asked. She could tell from his tone he was about to test her in some way.

'They're full of life.'

'They were all heroin addicts. Bad cases.' He stopped to judge her response. Lotte didn't say anything. 'I straightened them out,' he continued. 'Without me they would be dead. They are rich kids. *Figli di papa*. It's the rich kids in this country who become heroin addicts, not the poor ones.'

Now she knew why Felix hadn't taken her tip. He was probably in line to inherit a few million dollars.

'Commendable of you to help them,' said Lotte. It all fitted. A man who would be king.

Cosmo wanted to know more about Lotte. She told him she was married. Her husband, William, was an industrial designer. He reciprocated with the information that he had a girlfriend. She was away from the island that week visiting relatives. She was twenty-two years old, a potter and weaver. He would show Lotte some of her work tomorrow. Lotte was thinking unkind thoughts about older men and their preference for very young women, when he said, as if he could read those thoughts, 'I have tried to go with older women, but they are so...' he searched for the right words, '...scarred by life.'

You're a little scarred yourself, thought Lotte.

The talk turned to Lotte's work. They discovered they had someone in common, a woman writer now dead. Lotte had been her agent in the last years of her life. Cosmo knew the woman writer from a different

period, the years just after the war when she'd had a
house on Crete. He was distressed to learn she had
died.

'I was her lover, you know,' he said.

Lotte hadn't known. He disappeared and came
back with a photograph of himself with the woman
writer and her husband. Cosmo was looking at the
writer, she at her husband, her husband at Cosmo.
Lotte was right. Cosmo had been handsome as a young
man.

'Her husband was jealous, so jealous!' said
Cosmo. 'I called it off, but not because of him. There
was another problem. She smoked all the time, even
when she was taking a shower. And she drank wine
from early in the morning. To be frank about it, she
smelled. Love is skin to skin after all.'

He gave her a torch for the walk up to the hotel.
Lotte thanked him for his hospitality, and he wished
her a good night's rest.

'Are you sure you will be okay up there by
yourself?'

'I'll be fine.'

It was a gusty night. Small clouds scudded across
and partially obscured the nearly full moon. She was
walking along, pondering Cosmo's character, when a
man appeared out of nowhere next to her. She swung
around, shining the torch in his face. It was one of
Cosmo's staff. He said something she couldn't understand, but she gathered he meant no harm. They kept
company for a short way, and then he peeled off and
disappeared into a yard.

She passed the cemetery where the road was lined
with eucalypts. The leaves made a rasping sound Lotte
liked. Once in her room, she locked its double doors

on the inside with the key. There was a small bolt, a flimsy one, but she shot it across anyway, just in case. She undressed quickly and climbed into bed.

Lotte had been asleep for about half an hour when she was woken by a noise. Somebody had walked into one of the deckchairs on the terrace. Lotte jackknifed into a sitting position and switched on the lamp next to the bed. She listened hard. She heard nothing else. And then the double doors, as if someone were pressing on them from the outside, started to cave in slowly. Lotte was up and out of bed in a flash.

'Who's there?' she called. The doors stopped moving. She knew she should go outside and investigate, and confront whoever it was, but she couldn't make herself do it. Instead she dragged a large stone, used as a doorstop or ashtray – it had an indentation in the top – across the floor and jammed it where the two doors met. She backed across the room and waited. Nothing happened for a minute or two, and then the key she'd left in the lock began to jiggle. It stopped.

She crept over and checked the door onto the side terrace. It was locked. The small windows up near the ceiling had shutters. She climbed up on a chair and closed them. She went into the bathroom and latched the shutter of the window in there. Then she dragged on a pair of jeans, a sweater, Reeboks.

Did she have anything she could use as a weapon? William had given her a pocketknife, one with a bone handle. For peeling fruit, he'd said. She found the knife, extended the blade out full. It seemed so puny. She got back on the bed and sat there bolt upright – now she understood the meaning of that phrase – her heart pounding. She listened and listened. Soon she had a headache from listening.

Who could it be? Cosmo? Surely not. One of his sidekicks? An islander? Someone from the first hotel? Had somebody mistaken her willingness to stay up here as something else? She thought of her friend Daphne. She had been in Athens. A taxi driver, instead of taking her to a restaurant, had detoured to a dockside area and raped her.

There was another noise, this time from the small terrace on the side. It had to be the wind. It had to be. She couldn't believe this was happening. She was hollowed out by fear. She tried to unclench her hands but couldn't. Surely if somebody wanted to get in all they'd have to do is rush the door. Would the islanders down in the village be able to hear her yelling?

William. Too busy to come on vacation with her. Anyway, she had needed time to herself. Did he know where she was? She hadn't called to tell him she had changed hotels. She was going to do that in the morning. Did anybody else know where she was? The Englishwoman. Helen. She knew. Another noise from the side terrace. Oh sweet Jesus. That's it, a prayer, she needed to pray, that would calm her. She didn't know any prayers. Make one up. Let her go home safely. Please.

Now that she had shuttered all the windows, the air in the room was close. It smelled acrid. She looked at her watch. It was one o'clock. One-twenty. Two-fifteen. Perhaps if she read something morning would come quicker. She picked up Norman Lewis's book: *March 19. Today Vesuvius erupted. It was the most majestic and terrible sight I have ever seen, or ever expect to see. The smoke from the crater slowly built up into a great bulging shape having all the appearances of solidity. It swelled and expanded so slowly that there was no sign of movement in the cloud which, by the evening, must have risen thirty or forty thousand feet into the sky, and measured many miles across...*

She must have slept because when she woke light was coming through cracks. She was still sitting upright. Her neck ached. The penknife had fallen onto the floor, the book along with it. She went over, edged the stone away and opened the doors. Outside the world was pink, the volcano across the strait garlanded with mist. You need four eyes to see the beauty of this island, somebody had said at dinner the evening before.

Lotte felt foolish about her lack of courage in the night. It had been the wind. She scared too easily. She was about to enter her room again when something lying near the threshold caught her eye, a small piece of wire, bent in the middle. Her heart stopped. If someone wanted to pry a lock loose, this was the way they'd shape the wire.

Cosmo was waiting for her in the courtyard down at the waterfront. Breakfast was spread out on the table. Coffee, bread rolls, butter, jam.

'How did you sleep last night?' he asked. And smiled benevolently.

'Fine, just fine,' said Lotte.

'We all slept very badly down here. The moon is just about full, that's why, I think.' He was talkative for somebody who hadn't slept well. 'Did you know,' he continued, 'that people become werewolves at full moon in these parts?'

'Come off it, Cosmo,' said Lotte.

'Well, they don't actually physically turn into wolves, but they do howl at the moon and become violent. There is one of them on the island. The man who makes these.' He held up a roll. 'The baker. His family have to carry him off to Sicily and lock him up when the moon's full.'

Lotte couldn't take any more of Cosmo or the island, four eyes to see its beauty or not.

'I've changed my mind about staying.'

'You can't leave. That's silly.'

'You've been very generous, but I can't impose on your hospitality for a whole week.'

'It's nothing. If it would make you feel better, you can pay me a little. Under the table.' To emphasize his point, he rubbed his thumb and forefinger together and then put his hand under the table.

'No. I must go.'

'Where will you go?'

'Across the strait.' She gestured in the direction of the volcano. 'There are hotels open there.'

'You don't want to go,' said Cosmo.

'I do,' said Lotte. 'I really do.'

Samuel Beckett is Dead

I am in Milan, walking along Via Borgonuovo. It is winter. It has been raining. The pavement is puddled, windows shuttered. And I am thinking about – oh, I am thinking about all sorts of things, the cheeses piled to the ceiling at Peck's, a penknife in the window of G. Lorenzi's, a courtyard glimpsed several buildings back, when it comes to me that my brother, continents away, is drowning. I can see him quite clearly. He is sinking slowly in blue water, he is going down, drifting down, his eyes are closed, his limbs loose, undulating. The water is intensely blue, the color of a Van Gogh night sky.

. . .

Two weeks in Europe over Christmas? *Aren't* you lucky. Aren't *we* lucky? Milan, Bergamo, Paris. Lucky, lucky, lucky. The day before R. and I are to leave New York, we hear on the evening news that the State Department has posted a security warning. To mark the anniversary of the bombing of Pan Am Flight 103, terrorists have threatened to blow up another U.S. carrier. R. and I are booked on T.W.A. I chew my bottom lip, R. paces the room. We consider the odds. We have so been looking forward to this trip. The chances are slim, very slim. We would have to be unlucky.

. . .

On the plane we have seats near the galley and become chummy with one of the stewards.

'Do you worry about terrorism?' I ask him. 'The State Department warning...?' I trail off.

He shrugs. 'Security is pretty good these days.' Pause. 'Except for Paris. I don't like to fly out of Paris.'

'Coming back,' I tell him, 'we are flying out of Paris.' The steward considers this and then extracts a card from his wallet. He hands it to me. On the card is a prayer. It has been written specifically for air travellers, to quieten their nerves. It reminds them that God is, as always – how could I have forgotten? – flying the plane.

. . .

In Milan R. decides to drop in on an old friend of his, M.T., a wealthy gallery owner. The elevator opens on a vestibule lined with fragments of marble. R. rings the bell and gives his name to the assistant who opens the door. From behind a coromandel screen comes a man so lacking in flesh he could be constructed out of pipe cleaners. It is M.T. He advances, his arms outstretched, shaking his head in disbelief, smiling hugely, at the sight of his old friend. 'It has been a long time,' he says, and the two embrace. I am introduced, and then M.T. turns to the assistant and says, 'Show them around.' He secretes himself back behind the screen.

There is not much to show us. Like the vestibule, the room we are in is lined with fragments of marble, which are prettily coloured but not the works of art one would expect a gallery owner to have on his walls. The young man bends toward us.

'He is sick,' he whispers, gesturing toward the screen. 'Very sick.' He bends closer. 'He is dying.'

M.T. does not reappear. The assistant lets us out.

· · ·

We are making our way through the Christmas crowds near the Duomo when we are accosted by gypsies. One of them is holding out a newspaper at waist level, the blind for the thieving hands of her accomplices. I am incensed. Do they think I am so stupid as to not know what they are up to? 'Fuck off!' I scream. With my umbrella I smash the newspaper to the ground. 'Fuck off!' I scream again, and go to beat the nearest gypsy around the head. The gypsies cower. So does R. He is looking at me, his mouth a small 'o' of astonishment.

· · ·

Via Torino. We want to cross the street, but the light turns orange. A man on the other side decides he has enough time to make a run for it. He hasn't seen the taxi haring up to the intersection. R. jumps up and down, waving the man back. The taxi driver brakes, but, thump, it is too late, the man is on the ground.

Amazingly, he hauls himself to his feet and continues on, wobbling a little, toward the curb. A policeman and R. rush to his aid. The taxi driver is angry. He gets out of his car and shakes his fist at the man. I have done nothing during all this except whimper.

. . .

I am having coffee and writing postcards in a bar near the funicular in the old part of Bergamo. Someone has left a newspaper behind on a table. The headlines are about Ceausescu. Has he been overthrown?

'What has happened?' I ask the woman behind the counter, hoping she will speak some English. She doesn't.

A man overhears me, taps me on the shoulder.

'Ceausescu caputo,' he says, stabbing his thumb downward in a gesture of dismissal. Enunciating every syllable as if he were in an elocution class, he adds, 'We do not like Communists in Bergamo.'

. . .

On Christmas Eve, we go to midnight mass at a convent. We are told the nuns there, a cloistered Benedictine order, sing beautifully. We are disappointed, first by the church and its swarms of suet-fleshed cherubs with unproportioned limbs, and then by the singing, which to our ears sounds vinegary. You can't see the nuns. They are hidden behind a filigree screen, such as you would find in a harem.

. . .

I wake up in the early hours of the morning. It is my brother again. He is sitting in the chair under the window, and he is crying.

What is wrong?' I ask him.

'I have something to tell you which will break your heart.'

I clamour to know what it is, but his answer, when it comes, is unintelligible.

I lie awake, reviewing my life, its happinesses and disappointments. I fail even to begin to imagine the future. Finally it is morning. Christmas morning. Church bells, competing with each other to announce the glad tidings, ring out carillons of crazed sound. I open the shutter. The gold statue of St Alexander on top of Bergamo's cathedral is riding the crest of a shocking-pink sunrise.

· · ·

We travel to Paris on the fast train, Lausanne-Paris, phttt, three hours, nothing to it. The seats on our half of the train all face backwards. We travel to Paris, phttt, three hours, nothing to it, facing backwards.

· · ·

Samuel Beckett is dead. And Billy Martin, too.

· · ·

I buy a postcard of Jean-Paul Belmondo in the movie *Pierrot Le Fou*. It is a still from the last scene, the one where he paints his face blue and wraps yellow dynamite around himself and lights the fuse. Then he has second thoughts about dying. 'I don't wanna...' That's how his last words were translated in the English subtitle: 'I don't wanna...', but it is too late. Boom. Smithereens. We thought that scene a great joke, V. and I, when we saw the movie. We were seventeen. We smoked Gitanes and wanted to be

Jeanne Moreau. We tried hard to live lives that took place solely in the interval between the lighting of the dynamite and the explosion. I would have liked to have sent the postcard to V., but we are no longer friends.

. . .

'This place is a shrine to male sexuality.' We are in the Picasso Museum. I have gone back to find R., who is enjoying the paintings and taking his time, to tell him this.

R. gets his where's-the-exit? expression. Picasso is one of his gods. 'Most people don't like Picasso. He's too much for them. He tears them apart,' he says, by way of reply.

'He doesn't tear me apart. I'm bored by him. I'd bet most women feel the same way.' Here I try out a gallic shrug of disdain. 'They say men think about sex every seven minutes. These paintings are living proof of that.'

R. turns away.

'You don't want to talk about this, do you?' I say to his back.

'Later. I just want to look some more.'

. . .

Our last night in Paris. A treat. A feast. Belon oysters at Bofinger. We are dressed, ready to go, but we are early for our reservation. I switch on the television. It is the news. The first item up is a warning against eating shellfish, or I think that is what it is. S.O.S. S.O.S. S.O.S. is being tickertaped across the bottom of the screen, and the announcer says something in French I can't quite follow, and then the image cuts to footage of people opening oysters, you know the way they do in Paris, out the front of restaurants, right there on the pavement.

.   .   .

R. has been working on a collage. It is for M.T. He has cut up the tags from tea bags, wrappers on sugar cubes, tickets to museums, the ribbons off *salumeria* packages, to make a tiny, exquisite homage to his friend. When he finishes, he posts it off to Milan, fretting about the reliability of the mails, the amount of stamps he should put on the envelope.

.   .   .

Charles de Gaulle airport is swarming with security police. We passengers are all very subdued. For oysters at Bofinger, for choucroute even, we have put our lives at risk?

.   .   .

We are nearly there, Newfoundland is below. People relax, initiate conversations with their neighbours. I allow myself the luxury of feeling bad-tempered about the squirming child who has been kicking the back of my seat ever since we left Paris. Then the pilot announces bad weather at Kennedy.

The passengers stiffen again, and fall silent. We could be forest animals who have heard the crunch of a hunter's footstep. Planes are being rerouted, but not ours. With engines grinding, we circle New York for an hour in fog so thick it obscures even the lights on the tips of the wings. When the plane does land, R. and myself and all the others clap.

Yoo-Hoo

My brother leans against the refrigerator and talks, entertaining me while I do the washing up. He looms large in the small kitchen. Thirty-seven years old, he has only recently stopped looking boyish, assuming the muscle-and-bone bulk of a man which he wears uneasily, as if he were a gridiron player forced to keep on his protective padding. He reminds me now of our Uncle Clarrie, big as a colossus, or so it seemed to me as a child. I always avoided being kissed or hugged by Clarrie because he had damp lips and smelled of sherry. Booze killed Clarrie, but not before it had thinned him down and stretched his skin tight across his cheekbones. A candidate for the glue factory, everyone agreed.

We are in my brother's house. He lives in Sydney, at Bondi Beach. My brother is talking about an acquaintance of his, a woman who crops up often in conversation, I have noticed on this visit with him, as an object of scorn. From what he is saying now, as he leans against the refrigerator, derision causing his top lip to pucker and almost meet his nose, it appears she needs only the smallest excuse to take off her blouse or whatever and expose her breasts to company.

Why this bothers my brother, I can't imagine. Topless sunbathing is the norm these days in Australia. No doubt there is some etiquette attached to it, although there's precious little from what I've observed. A friend of mine, who like me lives in the United States, a prudish place when it comes to breasts, told me about a picnic she went on with her parents and assorted relatives at a Sydney beach. Her two nieces, both in their late teens, took off their tops. We shook our heads over this — a family gathering! — and then conceded it was a fine thing her nieces should be so at ease with their bodies. Like Masai on the veldt, we said, trying to keep the dubiousness out of our voices.

My brother's girlfriend, young, long-legged, blond, androgynous as a lizard, has joined us in the kitchen, so he turns to her and says, 'Remember that time? After the barbecue. Everybody else kept their clothes on. And there she was, parading around. The thing is' — here he became confidential — 'she's got paper-bag tits.'

Ah. I see. Paper-bag tits. I feel I should come to the unfortunate woman's defence, but she doesn't sound worth it, even taking into account my brother's bias. For example, I have learned over the past few days that she is trust-fund lazy, peppers her conversation with references to 'Daddy', and practically lives in the dining room of the Royal Yacht Club. On one infamous occasion, she was heard to say, 'If you don't have poor people, how are you going to have servants?' The relish with which my brother retails this piece of idiocy is such that he all but rubs his hands together and cackles, like the crone when she closes the oven door on Hansel and Gretel.

My brother remembers something else about the woman that annoys him. Her Paddington terrace house is stockpiled with things she has filched from hotels. This, my brother and his girlfriend agree, is unbelievably tacky, especially for someone who has as much money as she does.

'I'd never take anything from a hotel,' my brother informs us. 'That's really low.'

His girlfriend pipes up. 'What about the beach towel from the Kahala Hilton?'

Which doesn't faze him in the slightest. 'Oh, right. Just asking to be pinched.'

His girlfriend runs off to find the beach towel so I can see for myself. The kitchen, in a high-rise on Bondi's southern headland, looks out over a steep wedge of park and clear across another block of flats to the beach itself, hooking away to the north. In the park, a man is jumping up and down, encouraging his dog to a frenzy of yapping.

The beach towel is duly displayed, and I admire it, having thought better of a lecture. Take the issue any further, and we could be playing Scruples. That's the game where people amuse themselves by testing to see how dishonest they have become in their quest for upward mobility. The questions people ask themselves go something like this: You are in an elevator, late for an appointment. As the doors close, you glimpse someone running up to the elevator. Do you push the 'open' button? How about: You are paying through the nose for the privilege of staying at a hotel that supplies guests with gorgeous beach towels. There is no way a towel can be traced to you. Would you take one? Well, would you? Another: Do you lie to your analyst?

At the bottom of the park is a seedy concrete structure several stories high, the clubhouse of the Bondi Icebergs. In front of the clubhouse, the Bondi Baths, consisting of an Olympic-size pool and a smaller one for children. Beyond the baths, the sea, which fills the pools at high tide. Membership in the all-male Icebergs is earned by participating in swimming events held at the baths during the winter, when the water is cold enough to freeze the balls off a brass monkey, et cetera, for at least three Sundays out of four. For *five* years. Meticulous records are kept of attendance.

To open the season, the Icebergs throw blocks of ice into the pool, a ceremony performed in typical Australian fashion, that is to say, no ceremony at all. They saunter over, chuck the ice in, and then get on with business. If you are not watching carefully, my brother tells me, you might miss it. My brother is dead keen to join the Icebergs, but they are a cliquey lot. After showing up at their functions for more than a year, he was crestfallen to have the club secretary, a chap with gums like Popeye's, follow him into the sauna, and say somewhat accusingly, 'Haven't seen you around here before.'

Although it is spring, races are still held at the baths on Sunday mornings, and this is where we go when the washing-up is finished, at a trot down the steep path to the park, salt air slapping our faces, my brother and his girlfriend leading the way, the two of them dressed alike in T-shirts, baggy board shorts, and Converse high-top gym boots. His board shorts are patterned with a dead dingo lying on its back, legs sticking up stiffly, while hers have a chook running amok against a backdrop of rotary clotheslines. His gym boots are pink, hers canary yellow.

We'd gone down to the baths the day before, my brother and I, only to find them closed because of rough seas. We squeezed through the locked turnstile. Waves were smacking against the retaining walls and belly-flopping into the larger pool. My brother stood quietly for a moment, watching the waves with a concentration that surprised me, and then dived in. I was beside myself. 'Get out! Get out! You'll be killed!' I jabbered at him as he progressed up the pool, fighting the chop. To my relief, he gave up after only one lap. 'If you must swim, why don't you swim over there!' I said to him, pointing to the other pool, the shallow one meant for children. Right then, what with the wash coming over the walls, it wasn't so very shallow. My brother became a picture of disdain.

The only trace of yesterday morning's turbulence is the debris that has collected in the corners of the pool. A group of my brother's friends, men for the most part, with a couple of women tagging along, have already assembled in the stepped spectator area. They stand out from the other club habitués, who look to be dodgy racetrack types. In contrast, my brother and his friends are all Young Turks, movie and record producers, graphic designers, clothing manufacturers; those kinds of occupations. They drive Range Rovers and wear Commes des Garçons suits and shoes with Doc Marten soles. They have Frequent Flyer memberships, Zero Halliburton suitcases, DAT machines, Duntech loudspeakers, and airmail subscriptions to *Spy*, the New York satirical magazine. No flies on these boys, who are at this very moment pronouncing 'Honkers' – Hong Kong – 'in', and Japan 'out'.

I pull my terry-towelling hat down over my ears as far as it will go and watch the men in their skimpy Speedos gather around the pool in readiness for the races. They stand with their arms folded across their chests, heads to one side, faces hiked into a squint, shoulders slightly rounded despite physiques in the peak of condition, rocking on the balls of their feet. The more senior competitors brace themselves against the iron railing, the better to support their enormous bellies. It is as though Australian men become pregnant with their maleness as they age.

I am sitting a little apart from my brother and his friends, who are acting it up, punchy with good humour. They have a quick eye and ear for the absurdities of life. One of them is repeating a conversation he'd had in the sauna with a fellow who apparently wasn't feeling well. 'Can't drink like I used to,' he'd remarked to my brother's friend. 'Only had ten beers last night and jeez I feel crook today.' A burst of appreciative laughter. They only come truly alive, my brother and his friends, with each other, or so it seems to me, the eavesdropping older sister. They are too sophisticated to huddle around the keg at social events, as Australian men are famous for doing, leaving women to their own devices, but they segregate themselves, if only mentally, all the same.

The water is sea-green and redemptive. My brother says I have enough time for a couple of quick laps, so down I go. I hesitate. It is years since I have swum in a salt-water pool. Oh my god. The water is so cold I think I will die. I try to stroke normally but instead keep stopping to take deep, tearing breaths. My hair comes loose from its elastic and blinds me. I get out at the first set of steps. Walking back to the spectator area, I rub my hair with a towel to hide my embarrassment. 'Nippy, eh? That storm brought in a cold current.' My brother means to be kind. Later, he wins his race. Handily.

My brother and his friends have a favourite word, 'quintessential', which is why they have moved to Bondi or hang out there. Bondi, with its seaside stucco and fish-and-chips smell, is quintessentially Aust-ralian. At Bondi, if you have a mind to, you can revel in clichés. So when my brother askes me if I'd like to accompany a party of them to a dance that night at the clubhouse, where the music will be provided by an act specializing in Perry Como songs, I snipe, 'Aren't you taking all that quintessential stuff a bit far?' I go anyway, prepared to hate it.

And I do. There they are, the men from the morning's activities – my heart sinks when I see this – down one end around a keg. For the occasion, they have scrubbed behind their ears, slicked back their hair, and kitted themselves out in short-sleeved shirts, trousers with knife-sharp creases, and white shoes. White shoes are big with the Bondi Icebergs. In the middle, up on a dais, are the Perry Como duo, or the Two Artistes, as they are billed at the door, who augment their singing and guitar-playing efforts with a pre-recorded drum track. And at the other end, the women. They all have the same look. The one that says, 'If this is as good as it gets, what's the bloody point?' *Hot diggity, dog ziggity, boom what you do to me, it's so new to me...*

'Wanna dance?' He is a cool customer. Rather than wait for a reply, he grabs my hand, presses an Aqua-Velva-ed cheek against mine, and away we go, fox-trotting around the dance floor. He takes care that his right hand, the one that ordinarily would be pressed against the small of the woman's back, doesn't quite touch me. Despite this lack of contact, I find myself propelled with the same firmness of purpose a policeman might frog-march a wrong-doer to a paddy-wagon. No small talk, and a brisk nod is all I get as he heads back in the direction of the keg.

'Eddie's taken a shine to you,' says one of my brother's friends when I sit down. He is small and dark, of Lebanese ancestry, the court jester of my brother's set. An aggressive networker, vain as could be about the size of his Rolodex, he makes it his business to be 'in the know'.

'Really?' I reply, unable to be anything but sarcastic.

Undeterred, he continues. 'Eddie's the club Romeo, very active in the slap-and-tickle department. Rumour has it that he once lured some poor woman into the clubhouse, this exact room probably, and convinced her to make love with her head sticking out the window. One of Eddie's pals was hiding in the room, and they swapped places without the woman catching on. Eddie ran down the stairs out into the street and waved – yoo-hoo – at her.'

As sourly as I can, I say, 'That sounds apocryphal.'

'Why don't you take one of these with you? As a souvenir.' The court jester of my brother's set hands me a beer coaster with the Bondi Icebergs insignia stamped on it. *Never dreamed that anybody could kiss thataway, bring me bliss thataway, tell me where have you been all my life...?*

The next day, a public holiday, I go for a walk along the beach. Spring sunshine has brought out the crowds. There are plenty of bare breasts. Already some of these women have tans the colour and texture of cardboard. A man with a thick moustache passes another with a similar moustache and gives an admiring growl. At the water's edge, members of the Bondi Surf Bathers Life Saving Club are being put through their routines. I stop and watch a team of ten-year-olds, the strings of their lifesavers' caps knotted tight under the chin. The boys have clear eyes, and the girls, smooth, lanky limbs. An instructor blows a whistle, and they run out into the surf, high-stepping through the low waves like show ponies. The sun disappears behind a cloud. I remember then. About Uncle Clarrie. He was so big he could block out the sun.

J.D. Salinger and the Captain of the Hanwood Cricket Team

My father is at first slip. He is captain of the team. He wears flannels and a blue cap with an insignia of crossed cricket bats on the front. The bowler shambles toward the wicket. The batsman top-edges the ball, blips it into the air. One run. The fielders shield their eyes against the glare, but the ball falls uncaught. Another run. My father slaps his cap against his leg. He looks disgusted. He does a Walter Mitty and imagines he is captain of the West Indian cricket team, which has just participated in a celebrated series of Test Matches in Australia. The captain of the Hanwood cricket team signals his men in closer.

My father loves his Saturday afternoons. He can put away his shovel and gumboots and mud-encrusted overalls – he is a farmer in an irrigation area – and kit himself out in pristine white cricket gear. He is a quiet man, fair in his dealings, a good sense of humour, so he is well liked by his teammates. After the game they all repair to the Returned Services League Club for some beers. The club's air-conditioning and acres of carpet with clashing patterns are a source of local pride. Opposite the club is a memorial, a Fairey Firefly fighter-bomber – a real one – mounted on a pillar and giving the appearance of being about to make an emergency landing in the car park.

At the Saturday afternoon cricket match I have described, my mother is one of the scorekeepers. The other is the wife of the captain of the opposing team. Between pencilling in runs and tallying scores, they swap recipes for scones and sponge cake. They talk icings. They compare the quantity and variety of preserves they have in their pantries. My mother tells the woman about the trip we made to Sydney to watch one of the Test Matches between the West Indians and the Australians, how thrilling it was, how gallant the West Indians. The wife of the captain of the opposing team, who listened with her family to the Test Matches on the radio, does her best to hide her envy.

My only sibling, a brother younger by two years, is there that Saturday, loitering between the cars with his best friend, the wicket-keeper's son. They counsel each other in low voices about girls, how to lure them behind a toilet block or into an empty irrigation ditch and what to do once they get them there. They also discuss the recent Test Matches and how, if they had been on the Australian side, they would have thrashed the West Indians.

And I am there too, in the back seat of our car, a two-toned station wagon, a Standard Vanguard whose dinky futuristic curves will later qualify it, along with rope petticoats and coffee tables in the shape of a painter's palette, as an emblem of the 1950s. I hate the car. I hate this country town. I hate my mother and father. And especially I hate cricket. It seems to me that my teenage years are as interminable as a cricket game. I want to be far away, in a city where life is fast; faster than a ball bowled by Wesley Winfield Hall.

I am reading J. D. Salinger's *Franny and Zooey.* The first part of this novel takes place in New Haven before a Yale football game, the second in a large, shabby, memento-filled apartment in the East Seventies in New York. The apartment is inhabited by the Glasses, a voluble Jewish show-biz family. I am mesmerized by this book. I am a freckle-faced Australian country girl. My ignorance about the United States could fill swimming pools. Raccoon coats, martinis, and section men mean nothing to me. Apartments in the East Seventies are completely beyond my ken. I have never met a Jewish person. But I am Franny. To be more precise, I feel as Franny does, fed up to the gills with the stupidity of the world and everybody in it. So I emulate Franny. In the back of the Standard Vanguard I do what Franny does when she flees to the ladies' room of the restaurant in New Haven. I shut my eyes and squeeze the optical nerves with the heels of my hands. I see stars. And then, like Franny, I cry for five minutes, big violent sobs and ugly sucking breaths. God, how I wish for a wise older brother who will set me straight, a Zooey to my Franny. And no more cricket, ever.

This Saturday afternoon cricket game is different in appearance in some important respects from the ones played in England. There is no lambent sunshine, emerald-green grass, or spectators lolling on striped canvas chairs. Instead it is hot, very hot. Sweat streams from under the cricketers' wool caps. Their shirts stick to their backs. The grass, what there is of it, is singed and sorry-looking. Bowlers, batsmen, and fielders scuff dust into the air every time they break into a run. But the detail that looms largest in my memory is the light, the bleaching glare of the Australian sun, more pitiless and numbing than the illumination from arc lamps in the interrogation rooms of the KGB. You know the phrase, 'the play of light'? The light on the Riverina plains doesn't play, it is deadly serious, a you-can-run-but-you-cannot-hide light. There are no shadows, no undersides, no dark corners. An American society woman famous for her perfectionism has painted in the shadows in her country house in case the sun doesn't oblige. I understand the impulse. Right now, in my mind's eye, I try softening the cricket game I have conjured by painting in the shadows. I give my father a long one.

In the interest of presenting a tidy family portrait, not to mention one that serves my emotional needs and those of my imagination, I have painted in more than the shadows. My father was captain of the Hanwood cricket team for a while, but whether he was in the year I am attempting to evoke – the Test Matches referred to took place in 1961 – I don't remember. However my mother would not have been present. She wasn't one to make small talk with other women or sit around and watch her husband play sport. Like everybody else in Australia, she had been swept up in the excitement generated by the West Indian Test Matches, but her preferred sport around that time was car trials.

Car trials entailed banged-up, slogan-daubed

Holdens hurtling along highways and through country towns. People lined the route and cheered. Dogs barked. The best-known of the contestants in the car trials was Gelignite Jack Murray, so-called because he chucked sticks of dynamite out his car window. In my opinion, for this inspired method of livening-up funereal main streets Gelignite Jack should be canonized as the patron saint of performance artists. At the very least he is as deserving of a statue as the dog who sat on the tucker box. My mother participated in one of these car trials as a navigator. We children were beside ourselves at the prospect and proud of her but also worried. She would be gone for days and in the company of strange men. I wonder what my father thought.

My brother might have been at the cricket match and doing as I have described – he had a year or so to go before he was packed off to an agricultural boarding school where he learned to hate farming. But I would not have been sitting in the back seat of the car reading *Franny and Zooey*. Although the novel came out in 1961, it would take a few years for it to cross the Pacific and land on the shelves of our public library. When it did, I most certainly took it to my heart, along with *Raise High the Roof Beam, Carpenters*, the other book of Salinger's featuring the Glass family. However it wasn't Franny who I wanted to be; it was Zooey. Now there was a smart boy.

I could not have been in the back seat of the car practising being sensitive for another reason. On Saturday afternoons I played basketball. Men's basketball – not the confining women's version. My friends and I – we all went to the public high school – had put together a team. We had a yellow uniform which had a princess-line waist with a pleated skirt and the name of the team – the Yo-Yos – on the front in white plastic lettering and our team numbers on the back. Pounding up and down the indoor court at the showground, we were not above roughhouse tactics, jostling the opposing team's players, sticking elbows into their ribs, tripping them up if the referee wasn't looking. We were good. We trounced the Catholic girls.

All the same, I grew up in a great hurry to shuck my country self. The name my family called me – Cathy – was one of the first things to go. My wish came true and I now live in the fastest city of them all – New York. Not only that but in Franny-and-Zooey-land – in the seventies on the Upper East Side. When I first arrived in New York, I was homesick. I had been as desperate to leave Australia as I had that country town, but I was homesick all the same. I smoked Drum tobacco in those days. I'd roll skinny little cigarette after skinny cigarette, smoking them right down as far as I could, staining my fingers and my teeth yellow. This was not a popular way of consuming nicotine in New York, but I found a tobacco store in the theatre district that sold Drum. It was run by Pakistanis, and, as Pakistanis often are, they were keen on cricket. So homesick was I that I feigned an enthusiasm for the game and would spend half an hour at a time in the shop comparing Dennis Lillee's bowling prowess with Imran Khan's. I knew nothing about either cricketer but managed to bluff my way.

My father will be seventy next April. He plays bowls now. Early this year he had his phone service adjusted so he could direct-dial, as he put it, 'anywhere in the world'. As I am the only person he knows who lives 'anywhere in the world', I took this as a gesture of reconciliation after years of bad feeling between us. My father calling me to talk about the weather and how the trade unions are ruining the country delights me more than I can say. The phone rings, and there he is. 'Cathy,' the ex-captain of the Hanwood cricket team shouts, his voice top-edged off satellites. 'Is that you?'

DOLL

Doll is what is referred to as a 'big girl'. She is tall, nearly six foot, and amply built. She has black hair, white skin, red lips. Snow White's colouring. She has a plain face, but friendly, a tall woman's face, and is inclined to bruise under the eyes when she stays up late.

Men are attracted to Doll, although she seems hardly to notice. That is, she goes to bed with them, but as one would go to the movies, for entertainment. All her attention is concentrated on Doll, her plans and aspirations, none of which includes romance.

She does have a boyfriend of sorts. Miguel is as small as Doll is tall, and he dotes on her. The bond between them is music.

Miguel is a tenor saxophonist in a jazz band. Ben Webster is his hero. He is apt to hunch his shoulders, close his eyes, and say, 'Play it *pretty*.' Someone told him Ben Webster used to do that. If the outward surroundings of Miguel's life are lacking in hope, his inner music is not.

Doll writes songs. Ballads, blues, pop. She sings, too. Her voice is okay. Her songs, well… hard to tell, so much depends on the arrangement, the calibre of the producer, the singer's interpretation.

Doll supports herself as a waitress. She works in the members' dining room at the Museum of Modern Art. She saves her tips, scrimps, until she can afford to rent a recording studio so she can make a demo tape. Then she rounds up her musician friends and persuades them to back her. She packages the tapes with her bio and sends them out to agents.

So far she has only had rebuffs, but Doll is persistent. She is like a cat who has only one idea, to climb into your lap whether you like it or not.

Doll and Miguel dream, and not idly, the most touching of American dreams, of having a pool shaped like a guitar. In the meantime Doll lives in a tenement near the Williamsburg Bridge in Lower Manhattan, Miguel with his mother two streets away.

The apartments in Doll's building are typical of the neighbourhood. They have narrow hallways, sagging tin ceilings, flaking paint, uneven floors, a bathtub in the middle of the kitchen. They are islands, these apartments, lapped not by sea but by dirt. They are also freezing cold in the winter, suffocatingly hot in the summer, and the street outside can be as noisy as if a carnival were being held there.

Doll's best friend lives in the apartment adjoining hers. Enid. She is an aspiring playwright. Enid is not as serious about being a playwright as Doll is about songwriting. She mainly goes to parties, meets big shots, and does cocaine.

Enid's view of it is that she is networking. She speaks of the contacts she makes at these parties as being 'invaluable', or 'money in the bank'. One day she will put it all on paper, 'it' being her childhood in a New England mill town, and then riches and acclaim will flow in her direction like water out of a faucet turned on full.

Doll talks about Enid's growing cocaine habit with Suzanne, who lives on the ground floor. Suzanne, a photographer, knows all about addiction because she herself is a recovering alcoholic. She is in A.A. and also attends Adult Children of Alcoholics meetings. She has stickers on her refrigerator, little red hearts printed with A.A. slogans like 'Keep it Simple'.

Suzanne was a mess before she sobered up. Her friends are divided as to whether little red hearts on the refrigerator and a tendency to view alcoholism as the cause of all human misery are a small or high price to pay for Suzanne's new lease on life.

· · ·

Doll, Enid, Suzanne. I live in the same building as they do. I am older. Already I have reached an age where I am deriving more interest from watching other people's lives unfold than I am from my own.

I am a materfamilias figure to these young women. Occasionally I dispense wisdom – difficult to resist – but most often I just listen, which is more than they do for each other. Conversations between themselves are conducted as if timed with an egg timer. Three minutes for Doll, then it is Enid's turn or Suzanne's, back to Doll; while one is speaking the other is figuring out what she wants to say next.

I am fascinated by these young women. Their lives also sadden me. I see them as marooned in Manhattan by ambition. I often wonder what will happen to them. They have no roots in any community, no loyalties. They might get lucky and make the big time. Then again they might also be struck by lightning.

I have a crony, a bosom buddy. Her name is Rachel. We go way back. She has no patience for my young friends. 'They're lazy,' says Rachel. 'They think it is enough to have emotions.' And it is true that while their vocabulary for feelings is prodigious, their knowledge of history, geography, and politics is almost nonexistent.

Rachel is a union organizer and never was one to have much truck with the arts. 'There is no difference between those kids and Victorian women with their pianoforte and petit point,' says she. 'It is time women got serious about their lives.'

When Rachel gets going like this, I put aside my own reservations and come to the defence of my young friends. I point out, for example, that Doll is anything but lazy. But this story is not about Rachel and me and our wrangles. It is about Doll.

There is one thing Rachel and I agree upon: if you lived in this neighbourhood you too might dream of having a pool in the shape of a guitar.

. . .

To be famous herself or have her songs sung by someone famous, that is one of Doll's aspirations. And because she was adopted as a baby, the other was to know her real mother and father.

Doll was adopted by a middle-class Jewish family

from Baltimore. Her parents were as loving and caring as any child could wish. Doll can't fault the way they raised her. All the same, the minute she came of age, she applied for her birth-mother's address. When it arrived in the mail, she hid it away in the bottom of a drawer and left it there for several years.

I remember her coming to me and asking what she should do. She was not really asking. She had already made up her mind. Not knowing why her mother had abandoned her was eating away at her, she said. It was like having cancer of the self-esteem.

I pointed out that she could be opening a Pandora's Box of heartbreak and trouble. Doll said she was ready for anything.

'Cancer of the self-esteem!' snorted Rachel when I told her. 'She's indulging herself. She already has a perfectly good set of parents.'

Rachel had more to say on the subject, along the lines of there being two groups of people, those who grow up and get on with things, and those who take up permanent residence in the sandbox. You get her drift.

The address the adoption people had sent Doll was in a small town in Connecticut. One Saturday she hired a car and drove there. She told me that when she came to the edge of town and saw big white houses behind screens of leafy oak trees, she let herself imagine her mother living in one of them.

She would come down the path toward Doll wreathed in smiles. She would be wearing a silk shirtmaker dress and black patent leather shoes with grosgrain bows, the kind you used to be able to buy at B. Altman's.

Doll isn't overimbued with a sense of humour,

but later we compared this Hallmark Greeting Card mother with the reality and chuckled over it.

The address turned out to be that of a small general store in a scruffy part of the town. The store had a red neon Coors beer sign in the window. Doll sat outside in the car for more than an hour but decided in the end not to go in.

A year and a half went by. Doll screwed up her courage and wrote a letter to the address. Several weeks later she received a phone call. It was from a woman who said she was Doll's grandmother. She was chatty, as if there were nothing unusual about Doll's turning up. She told Doll that her mother – Beatrice – no longer lived with her, but she could set up a meeting.

Doll asked me to go with her to Connecticut the second time. It was winter. It was raining. On Highway 1-95, semitrailers were sending up curtains of grey water with their wheels. We were both on the edge of our seats trying to make out the road ahead.

I stayed in the car while Doll went into the store. A bell dinged when she opened the door. She introduced herself to the woman behind the counter, who turned out to be her grandmother. She was a fat woman, such as you find in rural areas, of indeterminate age.

She blinked a few times, assessing Doll, and then got down to business. 'Your mother had you when she was thirteen,' she said, pausing to gauge the effect of this information on Doll. 'She was no good, your mother. Right from the beginning, she was no good.'

'Who was my father?' Doll asked.

'She never told. Don't think she knew herself. More than one candidate.'

There was a knocking. It came from the back of

the shop. 'That'll be Beatrice,' said Doll's grandmother, and gestured for her to come behind the
counter. 'She'll be in the kitchen. Down that hallway.'

Beatrice was standing, sullen and stiff, just inside
the kitchen door. She had the undernourished body of
a woman alcoholic, pot belly, matchstick legs. Doll
went up to her, put out her arms to embrace her.
Beatrice smelled, very faintly, Doll reported in the car
going back to New York, of vomit.

Beatrice pulled away from Doll, sat down at the
table, concentrated on lighting a cigarette. Her hands
were a boiled red colour, the skin cracked. She was
unable to look Doll in the face. Her answers to Doll's
questions were inaudible.

Doll decided she had nothing to lose by asking
about her father's identity. Strangely enough,
Beatrice brightened at this question. Her eyes slid
around almost to where Doll was sitting. 'Sam Ketchum was your father,' she said, with the pleased air of
someone settling an old score.

Doll noticed that her mother had recently washed
her hair, perhaps for this meeting, perhaps for her.

· · ·

Doll's mother wasn't the only one in her family who
was 'no good'. Almost all were scrappers, lowlifes,
good-for-nothings. There was even a murderer among
them, her half-brother, Mick. Hearing of Doll's exist-
ence, he phoned her from the Danbury prison. He was
trying to find out if he could put the squeeze on her for
a loan.

'In jail for murder?' I have to admit my eyes
goggled when Doll told me about Mick.

Doll looked at the floor. 'He robbed an old lady.

Tied the gag too tight. She suffocated.' She was embarrassed, but I think more because Mick was a bungler than because he was a murderer.

. . .

'How's her self-esteem holding up under all these revelations,' Rachel wanted to know.

I told Rachel that as far as I could tell Doll was happy to have this ragtag bunch as her family. After all, they were hers and hers alone. Such is human nature.

Enid asked if she could write a play based on Doll's experience.

Suzanne advised her to join Al-Anon. 'You have to realize,' she explained, 'that when you are talking to your mother, you are talking to a bottle.'

Miguel said, 'Querida, I am here if you need me.'

. . .

Anne Ketchum, Sam Ketchum's mother, looked Doll up and down. Relief flooded her face. She started to laugh. 'You're not Sam's daughter. You're Duane's. The spitting image of him. They were both fooling around with Beatrice.'

Sam Ketchum, now the prosperous owner of a chain of dry-cleaning stores, filled Doll in on the details. He and Duane Tunney had been buddies in high school. Duane had been a rebel from day one, a real wild man. They were fifteen the year they were fooling around with Beatrice. Duane lit out soon after. He wrote Sam a couple of letters. He did time for passing bad cheques, then joined the army. That was the last Sam heard from him.

'Duane Tunney,' said Sam Ketchum, clucking

his tongue. 'I haven't thought about him in years. He was one son of a gun.'

.   .   .

Doll came to me and said, 'I've never told anybody this before. My parents – my adoptive parents – they were terrific, but I didn't want to be a good little Jewish girl. I don't know why. I just didn't. I started hanging out with the rough kids at school. We smoked dope, got plastered, the usual stuff. One day I went with two of the boys into the woods. I sort of knew what was going to happen. They tied me to a tree and they raped me. I was thirteen, they were both fifteen.'

.   .   .

'Coincidence,' said Rachel. 'You can't tell me it was programmed into her genes to get raped at thirteen by two fifteen-year-olds.'

'What about those identical twins they've done studies on? Separated at birth and years later they meet up and find their wives have the same first name and they both use Scope mouthwash,' I countered.

Rachel wasn't having it. 'She knew she was adopted. That was enough to make her feel different. She was acting out. Next you'll be telling me she has bad blood in her veins.'

.   .   .

Stillwater, Nevada. The window is level with Doll's pillow. Lying in bed, she can see three roosters balanced on top of a wooden fence, patches of long-stemmed grass rippling intermittently in the wind, a vast stretch of sand, mountains. The roosters had woken her earlier with their crowing.

Duane is up and about. Through the thin walls she hears the pop of a can of beer being opened, which means it is one of his bad days. Next, predicts Doll, he will put on *Blood on the Tracks*, and sure enough, ambling opening chords and there is Bob Dylan turning words into rubber bands, snapping them in your face or stretching them until they break.

Doll thinks her father is the most extraordinary creature in the whole world. She loves him totally and unconditionally, as a mother loves a child. She would do anything to protect him from hurt and pain, a quaint notion to have, she knows, in respect to Duane Tunney, Vietnam veteran, ex-member of the Special Forces.

At the airport, Duane was shy and awkward, as was to be expected, a father meeting his adult daughter for the first time. They started to talk. They discovered they had the same taste in music. Soon it was a torrent of words.

They have more than the same taste in music, she thinks, lying in bed that morning. They have the same nerve endings. She forgives him everything, for deserting her as a baby, for never bothering to find out about her. What else could he have done? He was only fifteen, for chrissakes.

· · ·

While Duane was at the American Legion Hall, Doll came across his military papers in the cupboard above the washer and drier. It was all there, the places he had been posted to, the combat medals, citations, ribbons, the breakdown, the discharge. Poring over them, she lost track of time and was startled to hear Duane's truck pulling up outside. She shoved the papers back in the cupboard, trying to remember how they were stacked when she found them.

. . .

'To look at him you would not think he had killed hundreds of Asians,' Doll wrote to me from Nevada. 'He is such a gentle, mild-mannered man. But he has troubled eyes. And he shakes. Badly. He is the oldest-looking forty-four you ever saw. He could pass for sixty no problem.'

. . .

One day they drove to Reno and Lake Tahoe. On another, to Las Vegas. Mostly, though, Doll and Duane sat at the kitchen table in the trailer and drank beer and talked. Tears slipped down his face whenever her return to New York was mentioned, and he would make her promise to come back. And then, having upset her as well as himself, he would try and cheer her up. He would sing, *I've been shooting in the dark too long, when something's not right, it's wrong, you're going to make me lonesome when you go.* He had Bob Dylan's inflections down pat.

. . .

Back in New York City, Doll told Miguel about her father. She was so happy, she was burbling. She went on and on.

'Chica, you are in love with your daddy,' said Miguel.

Doll slapped him on the cheek, a small slap. And then another and another, the slaps getting harder.

. . .

Duane told Doll many stories about his wartime experiences, but the one she chose to retell to her friends was this: It is April, 1975, and the Americans are evacuating Saigon. The helicopters, the Jolly Green Giants, are corkscrewing into the air from the American embassy. It is a crazed and desperate time. Duane is on board one of the helicopters. Also on board is a Vietnamese man who has an attaché case handcuffed to his wrist. Another American soldier, seeing this, leans over and suggests to Duane that they kill the man, cut off his arm, tip him out the door of the helicopter. They will share the contents of the attaché case between them. Duane says no. The other soldier says he will do it anyway. Duane has to knock him out cold to prevent him from killing the Vietnamese man.

'Can you imagine such a thing?' Doll would say when she finished telling the story. 'Can you imagine it?'

. . .

Miguel is jealous of Duane. Doll is also jealous of Duane, of his being a man. Doll would have liked to lived her father's life. Guns, guitars, and roaming free, is how she put it me.

'Sounds like a line from one of her songs,' said Rachel, shaking her head.

. . .

Duane calls Doll every day, or she calls him. She complains cheerfully about her phone bill. She also hears from her grandmother in Connecticut at least once a week. Mick keeps in touch, too, from the Danbury prison. Beatrice is the only one who won't have anything to do with Doll. Duane makes up for this disappointment a hundred times over.

Miguel doesn't come around anymore.

Doll has heard that there is a chance – admittedly a small chance – that k.d. lang might record one of her songs.

Doll's life is humming along.

WOMEN FALLING DOWN
IN THE STREET

Crocodile eyes shine red at night. They glow like coals. Some years ago I was staying at a wilderness lodge on Cape York Peninsula, the furthermost tip of Australia. Big man-eating crocodiles – 'salties', as they are called, to distinguish them from the harmless freshwater species – inhabit the estuaries there. After a dinner during which the management had spooked the guests with stories of how crocodiles can outrun human beings, I went for a walk. I was making my way along a path that led to a beach when I saw, at ground level, two little red eyes coming swiftly in my direction. Frightened the bejesus out of me, I can tell you. It turned out to be a foam-rubber crocodile rigged up with battery-operated eyes. The management of the lodge was playing a prank.

I was thinking about this incident, how I had fled squeaking into the underbrush, as I waited to cross

East Seventy-second Street near where I live in New York. It was brought to mind by the traffic lights. The sky was a greyish-blackish-blue colour, making the red of the lights more luminous than usual. Crocodile-eye red, or at least the red of the foam-rubber crocodile's eyes. I was cursing the management of the lodge for nearly giving me a heart attack – the intervening years having completely failed in helping me see the humour of the situation – when the woman standing next to me, through impatience or absentmindedness, stepped off the curb early, before the lights had changed. A car nearly clipped her, and as she jumped out of its way, she slipped. She fell backwards.

In her surprise to find herself lying on the ground looking up at the sky, she forgot herself and waggled her arms and legs agitatedly, as a beetle does when flipped over. I helped her up. She was wearing a grey coat with a black velvet collar, and her black pumps had a strip of gold metal between the heel and the upper. Her hair was short and carefully coiffed. A dull woman, I thought, as I hauled her to her feet. A dentist's wife.

I have never met a dentist's wife. For all I know they might be a varied group of females about which it is impossible to make generalizations. And I regard myself as an open-minded person. I consider myself as awake to prejudice in my attitudes as a dog is to fleas. And yet there it was. Before you could say 'banana skin'. Dentist's wife.

What would she make of me? Right at that moment, being dazed from her fall, nothing. She brushed herself down and then tested her shoes, scraping them to see if the soles were slippery. I suspect she hoped to blame the shoes for her mishap and not her carelessness in stepping out into the street. But if I were lying on the ground, would she have assessed me in a glance the way I had her? Cropped hair, no make-up, jeans, an arty type, left-winger, full of opinions, pro-abortion, anti-fur. Her prejudices and mine: I can see them lined up opposite each other, row upon row, like toy soldiers, armies of them.

I had only gone a block when I came across the second woman. She was already down when I found her, sprawled inelegantly on her stomach. She had misjudged the curbing, which is higher than usual at that particular spot, and caught her foot. Her lip was bleeding. Oh dear, oh dear, I said. Are you hurt? Can you get up? I put out my hand, but she ignored it. Just then a man came by, a technician from the telephone company. He was black. Can I be of assistance? he asked, and extended his hand. She took it.

She was in her sixties or thereabouts, wearing a fur coat, a long-haired variety, fox or raccoon. The fur was silvery blonde, and it matched her shoulder-length hair. She had that bewildered expression rich women sometimes get as they grow old and their looks fade. They don't have to open their mouths for you to discover their unhappiness. Their faces say it all: What's happening to me? Where's my life gone? Where did I go wrong? Her husband probably had dumped her for a younger version of herself, and she had been forced to move from a duplex to a smaller apartment and give up her full-time maid.

We fussed over her, the man from the telephone company and I. You must see a doctor, we said. She told us she had been on her way to keep an appointment with the doctor when she fell. She was dabbing at her lip with a white linen handkerchief edged with lace, we were making noises of sympathy, when I caught the smell of gin. As quickly as 'dentist's wife' had popped into my head, so now did 'dipsomaniac'.

Satisfying word, that, implying as it does not only giddy inebriation but furtiveness as well, flasks hidden in handbags, fifths in shoe-boxes. Remember Kay Kendall in *Les Girls*? She played a dancer who took pulls on the sly from perfume bottles into which she'd decanted liquor. Kay Kendall! I saw all her movies, *Les Girls, The Reluctant Debutante, Once More With Feeling*. She was a milky redhead with a long, thin, quivering ski-run nose, and a rakish charm. A darling woman, everybody said. She had an enchanted life, fame, acclaim, riches, even a happy marriage, to Sexy Rexy – Rex Harrison – and then she was diagnosed with leukemia. She was only thirty-two when she died.

I was tut-tutting Kay Kendall's untimely demise, but the woman who had tripped on the curbing thought I was still expressing concern for her. I'll be fine, she assured me, and squared her shoulders and launched herself down the street. It came back to me, something I had read in a biography of Rex Harrison. He didn't love his women; he adored them.

Set into the pavements of Manhattan are double steel doors. They mark the entrance to basements; goods and supplies enter stores and restaurants via them, and garbage comes out that way. When they open, they open up and out, and to avoid accidents, a bell rings to signal pedestrians to be careful. The third woman to fall down that day was several yards in front of me and right on top of a set of these doors when they began to open without warning. It happened as if in slow motion, the woman rising with the doors, and then tumbling forward.

It was quite spectacular to watch. I have always had doubts about the wisdom of stepping on doors such as these ever since I walked a poodle for a friend. He didn't just go around the doors; he skittered away from them. He felt the same way about gratings. If, as is sometimes the case, the grating took up the whole sidewalk, he simply sat down at the edge of it and refused to take another step. He couldn't be cajoled; that grating was as perilous as thin ice on a pond in his view.

You should sue, I said bending over the woman. She had gaping holes in her stockings, bloody knees. A fellow who had been unloading mineral water from a truck came running over. I saw it! he exclaimed. You want a witness? I'll be a witness. The doors hadn't opened right up. Whoever was pushing the button in the basement must have heard the commotion and stopped the mechanism. I peered through them. A black youth was staring back up at me. What do you think you are doing? I yelled at him. You could have broken her legs! The doors closed.

By now the owner of the restaurant – the doors belonged to a restaurant – had come out. He was fat. His eyes were expressionless. He stood there, his hands clasped behind his back, not saying a word. He was waiting to see what the woman was going to do. You should sue, I said again. Yes, yes, chorused the man from the mineral water truck.

She was young, the third woman, late twenties, early thirties, wearing a calf-length black mink. Calf-length black minks are the coat of choice among the smart set on the Upper East Side. House parties in the Hamptons, I thought, couches with scatter pillows with witty sayings in needlepoint on them, such as WE'RE STAYING TOGETHER FOR THE SAKE OF THE DOGS.

She had a plane to catch, she told us, and didn't have time to wait around to file a charge. Disappointed, I urged her at least to go into the restaurant and sit down, collect her wits, have a free cup of coffee. No, no, I must go, she said. The mineral water man shrugged and returned to unloading his truck. The restaurant owner went back inside, as impassive as when he came out. I accompanied the woman, who was still very shaky, to the corner, where she thanked me, and we went our separate ways.

Women from the Upper East Side weren't the only ones I was quick to size up that day. When I set eyes on the restaurant owner, XKE Jaguar, house in New Rochelle, wife who wears Ultrasuede, flashed through my mind like the slogans on Jenny Holzer's electronic message boards. However, you will have realized that my thoughts about my neighbours are sometimes less than charitable. Why do I choose to live here, then? A simple reason: you aren't always stepping over crack addicts or the homeless. Nobody pees in the lobbies or vomits in the stairwells. The last place I had, down in SoHo, somebody had painted signs on either side of the stoop. On one side, a circle with a bar across it in red, and in the circle, a picture of a man urinating. On the other side, the same circle with a bar, but in this one, a man defecating.

What can I say? This city feels medieval, portcullises and moats, marauders at the gates. Inside the gates! You hole up the best you can, and here I am, holed up with people whose values I don't share because the pavements are clean. I sneer at them and yet happily make use of the institutions – doormen, security systems, and so on – with which they insulate and protect themselves from unpleasantness.

The day turned to rain. The fourth woman was running to catch a bus. She was running and closing up her umbrella and signalling to the driver to wait all at the same time. She was wearing high heels, and one of them broke, and down she went. She fell as if she had been taught to fall, averting her face so she wouldn't damage it, hands out to break the impact. The umbrella and her pocketbook were sent flying. What was remarkable about this woman, what I remember most clearly, was that as soon as she hit the ground, her right hand shot out and scrabbled around until it had located her unattended pocketbook.

The fifth woman blew over. It was nearly dark, still raining, and a wind was gusting. The woman was very old, and weighed seventy, eighty pounds. A feather. A crowd gathered. She wasn't hurt. She told us her name, Mrs Morris Meyerowitz, and her address, which was only a building away. One of the men who had stopped escorted her home.

Mrs Morris Meyerowitz. Morris probably died years ago. They might be feathers, these old women, they might shrink as they grow old like wool washed in hot water, but they are as hardy as can be. The husbands make the money, father the children, keel over from heart attacks in their sixties. Their wives live on another twenty years, longer if they go to Florida. I wonder if Mrs Meyerowitz misses Morris? Did she love him? Would she have done as Ida Straus did? I had read an item in the *New York Observer* that morning, about a park dedicated to Ida Straus and her husband

Isidor. They were on the *Titanic* when it sank. When the call came for women and children to board the lifeboats, Ida wouldn't go. She folded her fur coat and gave it to her maid, saying she couldn't live without her husband. Would Mrs Meyerowitz have done the same?

More to the point, would I have? My husband is everything to me. I cannot imagine life without him. I lie. I can imagine life without him, and I am not looking forward to it. If we were in that situation, I think I know how it would unfold. I would volunteer to stay with him, he would tell me to forget the heroics. He would point out that he is older than me – by some twenty years – and has already lived a full life. And I would climb into a lifeboat. The other day he looked at me and said, Your hair is going grey, you are catching up with me. I will never catch up with him, our ages never will be in synch, and sometimes I can't bear it.

Are you still with me? Five women in one day? It happened! Now I want to change the subject, not entirely, but almost. I have a little sister, not a real sister, but a thirteen-year-old girl assigned to me by the Big Sister program. Her name is Maggie Ramirez, and she lives in a barrack-like housing project down near Wall Street. She goes to the Sun Yat Sen High School, where you might be interested to know they teach French and Spanish but not Chinese. I am supposed to be a role model for Maggie, but she couldn't care less about role models. What she wants is someone to take her to the movies.

Last Saturday I relented, and we went to see *Driving Miss Daisy*. Afterwards I tried to initiate a discussion. What was the movie about? I asked her.

Maggie looked at the ceiling. She looked at her feet. It was about prejudice, wasn't it? I supplied. Maggie nodded her head vigorously in agreement. I suggested that for practice we write a letter to her schoolteacher about the movie. This is what Maggie, with prompting from me, wrote:

Dear Mrs Johnson,

Hi! How are you? I am doing fine thank you! I just went to see a movie called *Driving Miss Daisy*! It was a very interesting movie. It was about an old Jewish lady who was prejudiced about black people and realized she was wrong. We should always think good thoughts about everybody.

> Yours truly,
> Maggie

Maggie had trouble with two words. The first one was 'prejudice'. P-R-E-J-U-D-I-C-E. I spelled it out slowly for her. The other word was 'truly'. No 'e', Maggie, there is no 'e' in 'truly'.

MISTAKES, TOO MANY TO MENTION

Philip. Yes, I knew Philip. I was one of the women who had their hearts broken by him. Or broke their hearts over him, a distinction that did not escape the notice of a famous Australian woman writer in a recent short story of hers. You might have read it. Some critics rave over this writer, saying she is Tolstoy and Jane Austen rolled into one, an awesome combination. Then there are those who think she is merely a passable short-story writer. Trust Australian critics to have opinions that diverge like railway branch lines.

Although I have not seen this famous woman writer for years, I have followed her progress. I feel compelled to admit on occasion I have nearly fallen out of my tree with envy at her success, even going so far as to side with those who consider her a passable short-story writer. I am not proud of this. No matter how you look at it, envy is a grubby little emotion.

What surprised me most about her story was that she did not bother to change Philip's name, something ordinarily done in the interests of delicacy, if not libel. We all know most fiction nowadays is thinly disguised autobiography. It is as if imagination has taken a holiday in the late twentieth century. All the same, I was shocked. You would think Tolstoy and Jane Austen rolled into one could have spent several minutes giving him a new name. I would have called him Bruce. Serve him right. Though most of us wouldn't admit it, to even up scores has its moments. However, the cat is out of the bag, and Philip will have to remain Philip, but I assure you everybody else's name has been changed.

I was Philip's girlfriend after Nellie, who usurped the famous writer. Nellie used to say that women fell in love with Philip because he had the knack of reflecting back an image of ourselves not as we were but as we wanted to be. Philip was also adept in bed, a cocksman, if you will pardon the expression. I once saw a Japanese drawing of a man being led around on a leash by his penis. Undoubtedly that was Philip, only his penis was choosy. It liked smart, articulate women who were putting themselves on the line for their sisters in oppression. Men like Philip were known as feminist sympathizers. While publicly sneering at all men, feminists had no compunctions about jumping into the cot with the Philips of the world. No other men were so foolish as to come near us. Later we got the bright idea of going to bed with each other, so that put an end to that contradiction.

The famous writer's story about Philip is one of those tales of rueful love in which women specialize, every heartbeat noted, every cruel word catalogued, often with a verbal skill that takes your breath away. The best-known practitioner of this sort of writing is Jean Rhys. Personally I think bleating in the night like a lost sheep is a waste of time. If I were to meet up with the famous writer now, I would say to her, as Katharine S. White said to Phyllis McGinley, *Why do you sing the same sad songs all women sing?* I was so impressed by these words, I immediately wrote them down in my bons mots book.

I confess that when I was younger, I read Jean Rhys. In fact, I overdid it, aspiring not only to write like her but to be like her. I have realized the error of my ways, thank goodness. Poor Jean Rhys. Did you see David Plante's account of a get-together he had with her? Young writer pays homage to aged legend. Apparently Jean had one glass of sherry too many and slid into the loo while sitting on it. She concertina-ed up, her knees hitting her chin, bottom wedged tight. David, David, she cried, come and help me! He pulled her out and then hurried home as fast as his two legs could carry him to write about Jean's undignified moment for all the world to gasp over. No wonder she died shortly thereafter.

Jean Rhys was not only a sot, she was crazy, failings I once sought to emulate. Some people attribute her crazinesss to all those unhappy love affairs she had, trailing around after cads. Others say Stella Bowen put a hex on her when Jean and Ford Madox Ford, Stella's husband, absconded together. The real reason, if you ask me, was Dominica, the Caribbean island where Jean Rhys was born and raised. I had the misfortune to take a vacation there, having in mind white beaches and crystal-clear water, and finding instead no beaches and festering jungle. I could easily picture all those vain Creole girls languishing on verandas surrounded by lurid flowers and going mad. I nearly went mad myself, and I was only there for a week. If Jean Rhys had been born in a more wholesome place, the course of literature might have been very different.

But I digress. When I first met Philip, I had a perfectly good boyfriend. He was a Marxist theorist who specialized in long-winded tracts about Althusser. I didn't understand a word he wrote, but he was handsome, with a shock of golden hair and honey-coloured eyes, tawny as a lion. The only problem was he lived with someone else, a doctor, so we had to sneak around seeing each other. Around the time I met Philip, she went off to America to become a Muslim. People did things like that then. At last we can be together, said the Althusserian. Too late, I replied. And do you know what he did, this tough-minded ideologue, this lionish-looking man? He broke down and cried. It is not often you see a grown man cry. But I feel it incumbent upon me to reveal he was also drunk. Everybody was drunk in those days, some more than others.

The famous writer described Philip as being beautiful. He wasn't as beautiful as the man I ditched. In fact, what comes to mind is his unfocussed red eyes. He had pale skin, too, so what he resembled most was an albino rat. But I didn't pick Philip for his good looks. The truth is Philip had cachet, and I was not without cachet myself, so the two of us together, or so we fancied, were a power to be reckoned with. We were big fish in a small pond. More of a puddle, really, as I later came to realize.

Philip's eyes were red from smoking dope. And

that was how it went with us. I was drunk, and he was stoned. Sometimes he was both drunk and stoned. I never smoked dope; it made me more paranoid than I already was. All our nights together ended in a brawl at four in the morning, either one of us slamming off into the empty streets of Glebe, in Sydney, where we lived. All kinds of silly-buggers went on, but I won't bore you with details. Let it just be said, mistakes were made, too many to mention.

The famous writer depicts Philip in her story as a footloose wanderer traversing the dark nights of the soul. I beg to differ. Philip was a hustler. He never had much money to fund his peregrinations, but he managed. This scam or that. Once Qantas asked Philip for advice on how to encourage young people to fly with them. What you have to do, said Philip, is cover your headrests with denim. For this sparkling idea, Qantas gave Philip six around-the-world airline tickets. Six! No wonder he was able to come and go as he pleased. After one of his jaunts, he came home boasting of having holed up in the Chelsea Hotel with Janis Joplin. This only increased his allure in my eyes. I questioned him closely about the Chelsea Hotel, getting the impression it was panelled with wood and hung with velvet drapes, so you can imagine my surprise when I finally saw the real thing, a seedy dump if there ever was one.

I suppose I thought I would be the one to win Philip, or at least have him stay with me longer than a year. Being Philip's girlfriend was like entering a competition. The woman he finally chose would be crowned the smartest and most talented of us all. But when my year was up, that was it, kaput, the end of me. I remember well the night he told me he was leaving. We had been to a pub, and I was feeling on top of the world. Philip was with me, so my cup ranneth over. Then Philip dropped his bombshell. He was going bush to live in a hippie commune. I wept. I pleaded. Philip stormed off into the night.

What I did next is completely incomprehensible to me now. I took an overdose. I used to do this from time to time, when life got a bit too much for me or a boyfriend wasn't cooperating. 'That's a bit extreme,' said one of these long-suffering gents after I landed in hospital in a coma. My tactics didn't work on him, but they scared the living daylights out of Philip, who had returned to find me lying unconscious on the floor in a pool of vomit. He made two phone calls and then left town on a Greyhound bus.

The first call was to a doctor, who approached my bedside as warily as if I were a cut snake. You'll live, he pronounced. The second call was to the famous writer. As a favour to Philip, she came around and kept an eye on me for a few days while I recovered. She was not yet famous, being in the middle of her affair with a junkie, which she was carefully recording in her journal. Later she wrote it up and caused quite a stir. Not surprisingly, I have never kept a journal. For that, you must take yourself seriously.

I did not see Philip until years later in New York. He had been there for some time; I was a recent arrival. He had gravitated to SoHo and TriBeCa where he and his cronies hung out in low-life bars, playing pool and drinking beer. He need not have left Australia to do this. I accompanied Philip to one of these joints. It was winter, and a giant fan blasted hot air into the room. The floor was covered with sawdust to soak up the spills. We were with Philip's latest girlfriend, an

American whose claim to fame was that she supplied cocaine to a mega-bucks artist.

You would have thought I would have been right at home in a dive in TriBeCa with an assortment of marginal people. But no. I felt square. A rube. I have since worked out why. What these downtown New Yorkers valued most was being affectless. Heaven forbid one display an emotion! Or use an exclamation mark. At home in Australia, my women friends and I cultivated our emotions as if they were prize peonies, so it was not surprising I felt out of place.

As we left the bar, moving through a light snowstorm, warehouses looming around us, who should we run into but Blue, an Australian rock-'n'-roll star known for his long tongue, which he thrust out during performances and lashed around in a supposedly erotic fashion. He looked like an ant-eater coming upon a plenitude on ants. Teeny-boppers fainted on the spot. Blue told us he was leaving New York to return to Australia. Can't make it here, I jeered. Got no balls! And so on. I can't remember how he reacted to this unwarranted attack, but I have since wished I could apologize. If the truth be known, I was quaking in my boots at the idea of living in New York and would have happily jumped into his pocket and hitched a ride.

As you can see, I had developed into a rather obnoxious sort of person. I settled into a tenement apartment in midtown Manhattan. Philip visited me there. I remember pressing upon him a copy of *The Way We Live Now*, by Anthony Trollope. I was in my Trollope-reading phase. At that time, I read all the way through the Palliser novels and right up to the last volume of the Chronicles of Barset. I put this book down on page 376 and never picked up Trollope again. I don't know why I stopped there, but I can recommend Trollope. The first thing he tells you about his characters is how much they are worth. In pounds, shillings, and pence. Very refreshing, that.

The last time I saw Philip, I had taken a job as an editor at an airline magazine, a position I thought beneath me, but I had to eat. He must have been in even more dire straits than I because he was writing a story for one of these magazines. So there we were, two Australian big fish down on their luck. We had lunch in one of those pocket-handkerchief-size parks tucked away in the middle of Manhattan. One entire wall was a waterfall. Over the roar of the waterfall and the traffic, Philip tried to conduct a conversation with me, but I had given up booze and was feeling very superior to Philip, who was in bad shape. His eyes were redder than usual, his skin whiter, and he kept twitching his lip over his teeth, like a horse bracing at a bit. Cocaine. I managed a few disdainful monosyllables, and then we went our separate ways.

On a visit home to Australia, I ran into Nellie, the girlfriend between me and the famous writer. She told me Philip had got married. The hypocrite! we exclaimed gleefully. How bourgeois of him! Et cetera. I am ashamed to say I experienced, in the furthest recesses of my heart, the tiniest jab of jealousy, an alarming throwback to that darker age. Then Nellie told me that no sooner was Philip married than he upped and embarked on a torrid affair with another woman. Well, we had a good laugh over that one, I can tell you.